I0741020

THE MISSES BRONTË'S
ESTABLISHMENT

THE MISSES BRONTË'S ESTABLISHMENT

Amy Wolf

THE MISSES BRONTË'S ESTABLISHMENT

ISBN-13: 978-1515160281
ISBN-10: 1515160289

First Edition: August 2015

Printed in the United States of America

Publisher: Ingram Spark

eBook published by Amazon Kindle Press

For more information, go to:
http://missesbrontes.com

To Charlotte, Emily, Anne, and Branwell Brontë

Special Acknowledgments

Sarah Laycock,
Brontë Parsonage Museum Librarian & Collections Officer

Janet White, for her French translations

The first duty of an author is, I conceive, a faithful allegiance to Truth and Nature; his second, such a conscientious study of Art as shall enable him to interpret eloquently and effectively the oracles delivered by those two great deities.

How can I bear my life unless I make an effort to alleviate its sufferings?

Charlotte Brontë, Letters

Contents

VOLUME I

CHRISTMAS 1843

There was no possibility of taking a walk that day. Flurries of snow still fell on the gabled eaves of Harley Street, deterring even the boldest carolers from stopping. Outside, all was as white as the Arctic, broken only by the huddled figure of a passerby. From my post by the picture window of our drawing room, I thought he might be an Eskomo or whatever those people are called.

As it required some effort to obtain an answer, I sat — or rather, *sprawled* — across a deep-cushioned divan, my muslin skirt assuming the shape of a downturned tulip bell. This led to some musing on the subject of belles (and their corresponding beaux), until the appearance of Alfred and Colin, two fine slim-figured men, who traversed the room's oriental rug to fight for a place before me! I gave what I trusted was a Sphinx-like half smile. Though I generally enjoyed male attention, I wished to remain close now, for these two were rather tedious.

"Happy Christmas, Miss Maria." Colin raised a glass of fine champagne in my honor. With his eyes as sparkling as the beverage, he managed to catch my gaze.

"Thank you, Colin. Same to you."

"And here's to a very happy new year." Alfred smiled through his long whiskers. Though not as handsome, he was by far the richer of the two and hence more worthy of my interest. Alas, he was stiffer than our PM Mr. Peel and bored (or was that "board"?) me nearly into somnolence.

"You're a bit premature, Mr. Goulding," I responded with a smile. Really, could they not just *leave me alone*? I felt as overstuffed as the giant goose we had just enjoyed. Sated by several helpings of mashed potatoes swimming in a buttery stream, along with a Christmas pudding, which, if dropped, might have crashed through the floor, I was in no mood to entertain.

It was Isabelle—of all people!—who saved me from further tedium. My purported "dearest friend," she was as great a coquette as du Barry, minus only the charm. I do realize, Reader, what a thoughtless child I was then. But what can one expect from an ignorant girl of eighteen?

"Off with you now, Gentlemen—shoo!" Isabelle waved the gentlemen away as if they were footmen. "We have serious business between us, do we not, Miss Shelby?"

I nodded, all too happy to see them go. I watched as they strode across the room, past velveteen curtains and the mantel crowded with keepsakes, just as Mother had last arranged them.

"So ..." Isabelle plunked down on a nearby sofa, bringing her curls close. "Who will you choose for a husband: Alfred or Colin?"

"Neither, I suppose."

"You are standing firm for something better! The eldest son of an earl, perhaps, or even a lord." She let out a boisterous laugh, breaking our clandestine mood.

"I hardly think such notables would be interested in *me.*" Father was rich, to be sure—*and* a Knight of the Realm; but union with the titled had been rare among the

Shelbys. Not for me such lofty aspirations! I was to be content with a rich merchant's son, like Alfred; or a rising barrister like Colin, who, at the Old Bailey, brought giggles in his powdered wig.

"Nonsense. With *your* delicate looks, you might attract a Prince Albert!"

"I daresay he is already spoken for."

In truth, Reader, I *was* considered beautiful, but so was almost every girl my age. I had fair hair that fell in ringlets; and eyes that had been likened to Venus's cerulean orbs (by Colin). I was blessed with an easy, appealing figure; and, when I chose to bestow it, a smile that could radiate warmth like our Yuletide fire.

Isabelle too was attractive, in her white, worsted muslin trimmed in near-lifelike flowers. She had a bevy of London admirers, while her thoughts were seemingly centered only on young men.

"Did I mention that at the Christmas Ball my dance card was filled in *twice*? All of my partners were pleasant—save for that wretched Judge!—but my present favorite is, I think, Mr. Whittome."

"Yet he is poor in health."

"What matter at forty thousand a year? The best doctors might be procured right here on Harley Street. Besides, were he to expire prematurely—"

"Isabelle!" I brought her up as sharply as my mare. *I* was shameful, I grant, given to pranks and mischief, but so far had not wished a prospective husband into an early grave.

"I know it is very wrong of me. Still—"

Our not-so-girlish tête-à-tête ended with the entry of my brother George. He was five years my elder, and, though handsome enough, I feared was something of a dunce. He had barely matriculated from Cambridge: had it not been for Father's influence, he would have found himself clerking at the railroad.

"Hullo. What can my sister and her friend be whispering?" He lifted a glass of gold sherry, which likewise lifted his usual dullness. "Ladies, name for my amusement your favorite present of the season."

Isabelle answered eagerly. She had not yet crossed George Shelby off her list of prospects. "For me, that divine silken shawl from India!"

George nodded, and I sighed as I answered. "I rather fancy the box of dark chocolates that Father procured from Belgium."

"Ha! Eat those and you will be as big as a Lord."

"George, hush," Isabelle commanded. But she did so with such a pretty reluctance that his heart—like so many others—passed into her jealous possession.

"Look! Look, what *I* have!" our sister Emma crowed. She was not yet twelve, and annoying in the manner that only younger siblings are. Now, she pirouetted in front of the fire, arms outflung like a ballerina, one hand clutching a black net purse, which contained an actual treasure: a small hillock of coins.

We all laughed with affection—it was Christmas, after all—as Emma's lucre caught the light of dancing flames.

"To us. And our continued good fortune." George imbibed a generous quantity of sherry.

"To us," the feminine quotient responded.

"And to a bloody smashing new year!"

"George, I'm telling Papa!"

"Hush, Emma," I remonstrated.

Her retort was to stick out her tongue which was still coated with peppermint. I knew it was wrong—it was hardly a ladylike thought—but I envisioned grabbing hold and pulling it out of her head!

"Ladies, Father beckons." George pointed his chin toward a large, whiskered man standing over the banquet table. At his side was a similarly large, blooming matron. She must have been smitten by the widowered Sir Shelby, whose heavy girth was surpassed only by his purse.

George, Emma, and I walked across the room, which could have—and had—hosted a neighborhood party, now filled with straggling celebrants. Father laid a generous table, as all Harley Street was aware. When we approached the still-groaning board, he politely asked his companion, "Mrs. P——, would you excuse us for a moment?"

As usual, I did not bother to learn her name.

Father motioned to the three of us—all that remained of our small family since Mother had died. Childbirth had taken her, and my memories—now dimmed by the hourglass of time—grew fainter with every season, for I had been but six. I remember a loving face, the lingering odor of lavender, but not much else, alas. Now as Father drew us aside, out of sight (and earshot) of his esteemed guests, I unloosed an involuntary sigh.

"Well, well." Father inspected each of us, and he seemed pleased enough until his glance fell upon *me*. My lassitude turned to fear, for I sensed what was forthcoming.

"Maria Victoria."

"Yes sir."

"I trust you have enjoyed your weeks at home."

"Very much, sir." I gave a low curtsy.

"Now that the festivities are expiring, I must address an urgent matter."

Emma suppressed a giggle. She and George were in their glory whenever Father chastised *me*. I am sorrowful to report that this was a frequent occurrence.

"What do you think I have here?" Father fumbled in the folds of his waistcoat, at last procuring from his pocket a crumpled sheet of paper.

"A letter, sir."

"Very perspicacious, young lady. And who do you think it is from?"

"The Misses M——'s Academy?" My voice was surprisingly soft.

"Just so. And what do you imagine it says?"

"She's been sacked from another school!" Emma crowed with joy.

"Not again, Sister. You have been expelled more times than *I* was at Cambridge!"

"Lower your voice, George," Father cautioned. In his view, the worst that could happen would be for family misfortune to carry beyond these walls. To him, the Shelby name was sacrosanct.

"Father, I can explain—" Actually, I could not, but I was a quick prevaricator.

"Let us review some sundry—for lack of a better term—'high spots.'" Father cleared his throat, then read in hushed tones: "'Conduct unbecoming a young lady of her station—'"

"I heard she dumped a bucket of water on old Miss M——'s head!" Emma broke into squeals as George clucked in dismay like a chicken. Sometimes—well, *oftentimes*—I wished I were an only child.

"Ah, here is a nice one." Father traced the feminine hand with his finger. "'Displays complete defiance to learning of any sort.'"

George wiped his eyes in merriment while Emma bounced up and down as if to launch herself into the ether.

I decided it was high time to mount a defense. "Father, they were teaching us utter nonsense, like grammar and how to add. What use have *I* for such knowledge?"

His response was a black look. "I will *not* house another simpleton like this gentleman here."

George looked befuddled. "Beg pardon?"

Father turned back to me. "You will *not* be permitted to sleep the day away, dreaming of nothing but frocks! You must acquire some semblance of learning. Nothing formal, mind you. Just a smattering so you can talk sense to your husband."

I tried looking pretty and pathetic. On Father, this usually worked to great effect, but he was having none of it.

"How many girls' schools have expelled you?"

"This is number six," Emma volunteered.

"No London academy will have you."

"Papa, is Maria going to Paris? Is she?"

"No, Emma, nor anywhere else on the Continent. But she is going *somewhere*, to be sure."

Clouded vistas of places I had never visited—Manchester, Dublin, Edinburgh—crowded into my head.

"Let us see what I have here." Father reached back into his pocket, withdrawing a modest, printed card in not-quite-pristine condition. He held it before me, and I read with increasing horror:

**THE MISSES BRONTË'S ESTABLISHMENT
FOR
THE BOARD AND EDUCATION
OF A LIMITED NUMBER OF
YOUNG LADIES,
THE PARSONAGE, HAWORTH,
NEAR BRADFORD.**

TERMS.

Board and Education, including Writing, Arithmetic, History, Grammar, Geography, and Needle Work, per Annum. 035

French

German each per quarter.

Latin

Music each per quarter.   1 10

Drawing

Use of Piano forte, per Quarter.   0 50

Washing, per Quarter.   0150

Each Young Lady to be provided with One Pair of Sheets, Pillow Cases, Four Towels, A Dessert and Tea-Spoon.

A Quarter's Notice, or a Quarter's Board, is required previous to the Removal of a Pupil.

"What?" I gasped.

Emma and George craned forward.

"What's '*Hay*-worth,' Papa?"

"Emma, that is '*How*-worth,' child."

"And how much *is* it 'worth'? A mere thirty-five pounds! Quite the bargain, after your other schools, Maria."

"Bradford?" I whispered.

"Ho, that's down south, is it not, Father?"

"No, My Son the Scholar. It is north. Rather far north. In the Pennines of Yorkshire."

"York—" I could not get the full word out.

"Hey now, that's good fun. Don't they talk like this: 'Gettem them childers and hoo aught brass'—or something."

I actually felt faint—I, who had never seen a vial of smelling salts.

"Who . . . are . . . these 'Bronts'?" I asked.

"I believe the proper pronunciation is 'Bron-tay.'" Father gave what I can only describe as a malevolent grin. "They are a family of spinster sisters—clergyman's daughters, in fact—highly accomplished, from what I understand from Mrs. P——."

"And what does Mrs. P—— know of it?" My passions rose hot in the face of this proposition.

"Hmmm." Father looked abstracted. "Her niece received this card from a cousin who obtained it from a relation of Miss Ellen Nussey of Rydings. The Nusseys are a fine old Yorkshire family and they may be trusted implicitly, per Mrs. P——'s mother. I have written to and received a response from the Reverend Mr. Patrick Brontë, and find myself satisfied as to all the particulars. To Haworth you will go."

"Please." I held out a braceleted arm, entreating as if for my life. "Haworth. And Yorkshire. Might as well be the wilds of America, with its saloons, shootouts, and savages!"

"I cannot be moved, Maria. You have been granted six opportunities, and six times you have failed."

Something about "seven and seven" revolved through my fevered brain, but in Sunday School, I had never listened to the teacher.

"I know little of the North!" I cried. "And what I do know is frightful. It is rough, industrial, cold. The inhabitants are coarse and unmannered. How little culture must there be!"

"Perhaps the lack of diversion will spur you toward further accomplishment. When you return to my house, I expect you to draw tolerably and play Chopin on the pianoforte."

"No, no," I sobbed, dropping to my knees in supplication. "Father, do not consign me to this fate. I promise to study day and night if I can but remain in London."

He assisted me to my feet.

"Three times is a charm, my dear, and you have used yours twice over. I will not tolerate among the Shelbys a disobedient child. Especially one of your sex. That is all."

He turned and shut the drawing-room doors behind him. To my naive young ears, it sounded like the ring of a guillotine.

TO HAWORTH

It was not to be a happy Christmas after all. After my trial and sentencing, I fled to the stillness of my room, seeking comfort in repose. I had never been overly devout—in truth, sermons put me into a stupor—but now, I sank to my knees at bedside and uttered a simple prayer.

"Dear Lord, I beg You, if You have any mercy at all, do *not* remand me to Haworth! Anywhere, anywhere but there! Thank you. Amen."

Apparently, the Lord did not hear sinners, or not those of my ilk. On Boxing Day, Father informed me that the Haworth term started shortly and I would need time to acclimate. (To what? Savagery?) This left but two short days to pack. At least, according to the notice, I would be spared the task of supplying towels and a teaspoon. I laughed and my laugh was bitter.

I instructed my maids to pack my gowns into a set of matched trunks. I would not spare myself any convenience, even in darkest Exile. It was my fervent hope that Bradford might host a ball or two. One must be prepared.

The next day, Isabelle called in person to proffer a teary good-bye. I rather wished that she had not.

"Oh dearest Maria, how *shall* I get on without you? The mere thought of your parting is bleak beyond repair."

"I am confident you will survive."

Yet despite her dabs of handkerchief and words of consolation, I noticed the occasional smile playing about her lips. Indeed, my absence would permit her to ensnare still more young men—more hearts to be taken like a tiger in the East.

"You will write every day, of course. Do not omit *a single detail.* I am beyond curious as to the dress and manner of these Bronts."

"It is *Brontë*," I replied, pointing out the petticoats, corsets, and chemises I would require for my journey.

"Are they handsome women, do you think?"

"I highly doubt it. They are spinsters and school teachers. Father said they are all rather young, though."

"No competition, one hopes."

I had not yet considered this prospect.

"And where did these Bronts get their learning? From the local charity school?"

For some reason, I rose to defend them, perhaps to raise my own role as pupil. "On the contrary. The two eldest studied in Brussels, and the other was a longtime governess."

"Governesses! Ha! They exist to be tormented."

"It is *I* who will undergo torment," I said, out of the maids' earshot.

After a tearful succession of kisses, pressing of hands, and adieux, my friend took her leave. Isabelle was basically decent, but more shallow than Father's fish pond. I was not sorry to see her go.

The day of my departure rang in cold and clear. I had already said my good-byes to Emma and Father at home. I could tell from the latter's expression that further pleas would be useless.

George and I set out in our carriage making for London Bridge station. In those days, the railway was still a novelty: an adventure to be savored. For this journey, my trunks had been sent ahead, so we were able to board our private coach without further encumbrance.

I sat on the cushioned seat, smoothing my skirt demurely, and surveyed my brother's countenance. I bore him no ill will but fully comprehended his role: he served as Protector, yes, but also stern Jailer. Even without his presence, I knew I could not run, nor could I disobey Father. Such was the position of our sex in those days—and as I write this, still is.

"Ho, here she goes!" George cried, as we departed amid a swirl of smoke and the harsh toot of a whistle. We had fully *eleven* hours ere we arrived in Leeds, at that time the closest terminus in Yorkshire.

We made out well on the journey, for Cook had supplied a cold supper and a container of wine. George remarked on this and that—the falling snow or a lonely cow gazing mournfully—but I, being in a storm of my own, had little interest in scenery.

At last, we arrived at Leeds.

"Beg pardon, bur 'ood theur be Mr. 'n Miss Shelby?"

A polite coachman greeted us and beckoned to a waiting carriage. Two footmen struggled with my luggage, handing it up so that it sat atop the black roof. At least Father had thought to provide for this one small courtesy. George said he had arranged transport with an inn, and the accommodation proved adequate.

By the time we arrived at Keighley, I was beyond fatigued. Even George seemed to dispense with some of his traveler's zeal. As the footmen removed my trunks through the magic of brute strength and sliding, I tightened my winter coat about my shoulders.

"Are we to be met?" I asked George.

"Well . . ." He glanced around. "I understood that the Brontës would be here to greet us, but I see no sign of a carriage."

"Ha—these governesses come by the clergy. They will appear in a hay cart or astride some mangy nag."

George laughed, his breath now visible.

The snow fell less than lightly as we huddled near the warmth of the horses. I noted a precipitous drop in temperature compared to the friendly South. I half expected to see Eskomos descending the nearby hills.

"How unspeakably rude to leave us outside in the cold." I felt the frigid air start to assault my extremities. Even my mittened hands were beginning to stiffen and numb.

"A moment. I think I see someone coming." George squinted into the hazy white glare that now enveloped our world.

A seeming apparition slowly came into view. Through curtains of white emerged two figures: one dark-haired and tall; the other fair and of medium height. As they approached, I thought to myself, *the smaller is really quite pretty.*

It was this person who stepped forward while the other languished behind.

"Good afternoon," she said. "Many apologies for our delay. It took a bit more time than usual to walk across the moor."

George and I did a double take worthy of the stage. With effort, we quelled any vocal outburst.

"I am Miss Anne Brontë, and this is my sister Miss Emily." She gestured toward the tall one. "We heartily welcome you to Keighley. You are our very first pupil. In point of fact, our *only* one."

I remained mute as Philomela.

George stepped up in my stead. "Glad to make your acquaintance. I am Mr. George Shelby and this is my sister Miss Maria."

Anne gave a graceful curtsy. Just then, Emily deigned to speak. Without preamble, she said, "Enough standing about. We must get home while there still is light." With that brusque introduction, she turned on her heel and left.

Anne seemed unfazed. "You must forgive my sister. She is not of what one might call 'a sociable nature.'"

My eyes widened, but not at the other Miss Brontë's rudeness. "Surely it is not your intent to *walk* back to Haworth?"

"Oh yes, it is but four miles. If we set out now, we shall arrive just before nightfall."

"And my things?"

I pointed toward the jumble of trunks, strewn on the ground in a pyramid. I had not realized until that juncture that there were fully *six*.

"Yes." Anne stared at the leather edifice as if it might attack her. "I fear they must wait till morning, when a cart may be summoned. This carriage is far too large to navigate our narrow paths."

The footmen began to drag my possessions into the railway station. The coachman looked relieved. "When they're done, we'll just be gerrin along then." He tipped the brim of his tall black hat.

"A moment." If someone was going to curb this madness, it appeared it would have to be *me*.

"Unloose this horse," I ordered, pointing to the rear left gelding.

"Soz, Miss?"

"Unharness him. I guarantee that my father, Sir Selby, will compensate you for the loss. You can tie his partner to the rear and make your way back to Leeds with a 'coach-and-two.'"

"What are you about, Maria?" George seemed overwhelmed by the complexity of my plan.

"Hush," I told him.

After a moment of balking, the coachman followed my command. A huge draught horse now stood before me, jet black and seventeen hands.

"Name's Balthazar," I was informed.

I approached my smallest trunk, unlocking it briefly to seize some necessary items. After my work was done, I securely affixed the lock.

"Won't you give me a boost?" I asked George.

He did, and in a moment I had mounted, both legs swung awkwardly over the beast's right flank.

"Miss Anne, would you mind?"

She looked rather terrified, but grabbed Balthazar's very long reins, bunching them up in her small gloved hands.

"To Haworth, if you please. Good-bye, George."

He gave a last wave, then vanished into the carriage. What a tale he would have for the denizens back home!

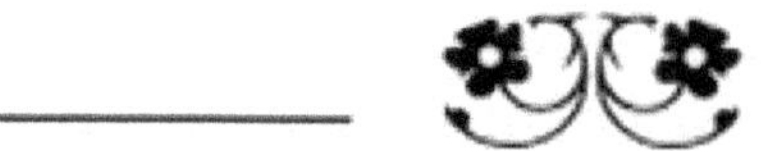

This was my first real glimpse of the Yorkshire moors, but on this trip, I saw very little. Snow obscured the low, rolling hills; the foliage (if there was any); and the very path we trod.

My companion and I could just make out a lanky figure ahead of us: Emily. Finally, she halted until we materialized at her side. Upon my mounted appearance, she doubled over with laughter, guffawing like a man.

"Anne, is she not a very Princess of Gondal? A queen, sitting sidesaddle! I shall call her 'Victoria.'"

"Emily!" Anne admonished.

Even though Miss Brontë's speech was odd, it did not concern me unduly. After all, my given middle name was in fact "Victoria."

Despite the gushing snow, I began to enjoy my strange odyssey. Warming up atop Balthazar, I noticed that the two Brontës minded the cold no more than a Viking.

Emily took the reins as we approached the frosty outline of a building. Not many candles were lit, but I spied a close-in graveyard, its vaults and uneven tombstones made faerielike by December. The northern sun was low when we finally halted. I leapt prettily to the ground (I thought) before a gabled door.

"I'll tether the beast by Victoria and Adelaide." Emily disappeared into the murk. I feared that the two she named might be actual personages, forced by the strange Miss Brontë to reside out of doors!

"Please, do come in." Anne made a welcoming gesture. I found myself in a narrow entranceway, separating what (to me) were two smallish rooms. I relaxed, moving gratefully to the right, into the study with its fire. I was reassured that though the Parsonage was not a palace, it was hardly a savage's den. What struck me upon first glance was the inordinate neatness of the place.

As I removed my hat, coat, and shawl, an old white-haired gentleman stepped spryly into the room.

"Welcome!" he said, grasping my hand warmly. He had a decided Irish accent, but his most notable aspect was the cravat—*or cravats?*—wrapping their way round his throat as if he were partially mummified.

"I am Reverend Brontë, and you are of course Maria. Forgive my familiarity, but this is a family enterprise, and not one to put on airs."

"Please sit," Anne entreated, gesturing across the hall to the dining room. I took a seat at the table and was soon joined by her, Emily slamming in from the cold, a queer red-haired young man, who bounded down the stairs, and another, who was perhaps the strangest seeming of all. She entered from what I assumed was the kitchen, followed by an elderly woman bearing a laden tray. The former was so diminutive as to be almost dwarfish—I had never seen a woman so small. What I remember from this first meeting was the plainness of her dress and her square face and reddish complexion. But mainly her large, dark eyes, which smoldered behind her wire eyeglasses.

"Good evening." She seemed at the same time shy and very composed. "I am Miss Charlotte Brontë. Welcome to the Parsonage. You must suffer from inanition, so please join us for a late supper."

I was in fact fearfully hungry and dug into the food with alacrity. I gathered, from the heat on Miss Brontë's cheeks, that she had played a role—perhaps the leading one—in preparing our simple meal. Though I was used to sumptuous fare, never had a plain roast, boiled potatoes, and pie tasted so savory.

"How do. I'm Branwell!" proclaimed the red-haired gentleman across from me. He had a small pointy beard and glasses, and could not have been far from five-and-twenty. "From Londinium, are you?"

I recognized the first part. "Um, yes."

"Harley Street, is it?"

I nodded.

His eyes misted over. "How I would love to visit that town one day."

"It is but a train ride away."

He sighed. "What a journey ye must have had."

"It was long, to be sure."

"And wintry." At that moment, his face darkened and his voice rose like an actor's. "'Blow, winds, and crack your cheeks! rage! blow!'"

Anne smiled and, losing her shyness, interjected: "'You cataracts and hurricanes, spout / Till you have drench'd our steeples, drown'd the cocks!'"

Which led Emily to declaim boldly: "'You sulphurous and thought-executing fires, / Vaunt-couriers to oak-cleaving thunderbolts—'"

"'Singe my white head! And thou, all-shaking thunder, / Strike flat the thick rotundity o' the world!'" The last lines were delivered by Charlotte in what I can only describe as a rapture.

I looked round in astonishment, a forkful of potatoes halfway to my lips.

"*Lear*, act three, scene two. Lover of Shakespeare, are you?" Mr. Brontë asked.

"No. He— is immoral, is he not?"

Anne and Charlotte looked down, trying to keep their composure, but Emily laughed so hard that liquid filled her dark eyes.

"Sweet Jesus!" Branwell exclaimed.

"Brannie!" Anne and Mr. Brontë rejoined.

I froze, feeling as if I had been lifted by the gods and hurled, like Neptune's trident, straight into the sea, to be ensnared by the watery king and his half-fish court.

The rest of the suppertime discourse went straight over my head: there were mentions of Byron, Scott, and the Duke of Wellington. As I went through the motions of eating, I thought, *these people are utterly alien*. Yet I could no longer cling to my southern condescension. In sheer power of mind, I was a newborn minnow and they were monstrous whales.

EXILE

My trunks indeed arrived the next morning, hauled up the cobblestoned street via a rough country cart. Its operators cursed loudly as they flung my luggage into a tiny back bedroom designated as "mine."

I had passed a difficult night. I managed to make do with my few items, but it was far from easy going. The wind had whipped ceaselessly in the moors beyond my window, and—even covered with extra blankets supplied by the thoughtful Anne—I still felt as numb as Ross achieving the Pole.

With my belongings beside me, my spirits lifted considerably as I prepared to dress for breakfast.

BLAM! BLAM!

The sharp report of a nearby pistol sent me backward onto my bed. In a hurry I made myself decent, sprinting down the narrow stairs to run headlong into Branwell!

"Whoa there! Steady. That's just the old man discharging his pistols—he does so every morning."

I disentangled myself from his person, striving to achieve composure. When I thought I had mastered myself, I still heard a faint quaver in my voice.

"May I ask as to why?"

"To see if they work, I suppose."

I waited for him to descend, then gratefully sighted all of the sisters at breakfast.

"Ah, Maria. We trust you had a restful night?" Anne was clearly the most gracious of the three.

"Yes, I thank you. Until this morning's Waterloo."

Charlotte smiled and Emily laughed.

"Papa will thank you for that," said Anne. "*That* is his favorite battle."

"He even scoured the field itself," said Charlotte. "On our first journey to Brussels." Something about this pronouncement seemed to depress her greatly, for she stared down at her plate.

The same elderly, white-haired woman I had perceived the prior eve banged in from the kitchen. Compared to her venerable years, Mr. Brontë was a mere stripling.

"Yo'll not be clemmin' i' dis 'ouse!" she said to me. "Or yo' had ma brass tha brains. "Nip on ahead, ea' naw."

She placed a small bowl of oatmeal porridge before me.

"By t' way. uz nem is Tabitheur, bur theur can call uz Tabby."

"How do you do, Tabitha?" I asked in my best London manner.

To Emily: "Get eur load o' dis 'un! Soon we'll orl be curtsyin 'n callin 'a 'Princess.'"

"I've already crowned her Victoria Augusta Almeda!"

"Emily!" cried Anne and Charlotte. The former gave her a warning glance.

"Brannie, why not escort Miss Maria out of doors? The air will do her good." I concluded then that *Charlotte* was the one who managed her siblings.

"I accede to Genii Tallii's every command!" Branwell bowed low. "Miss Maria, fetch your finest wolf pelt and follow!" He ran headlong out the Parsonage door.

After donning my thickest raiment, I succeeded him into the garden. It had ceased snowing for a time, and in the pale light of morning, I could see the Parsonage clearly. It was hewn from grey stone, with five curtained windows peeking out from the upper storey. It showed its age clearly, but was not ancient—perhaps built in the prior century. Compared to 30—— Harley Street, it was little more than a box; on its own merits, however, it was a spacious domicile.

I walked at my fastest clip to catch up to Branwell, who had turned sharply to the right.

Upon seeing me, he exclaimed: "Lo, there she be."

I laughed. This young man—with his unkempt hair and Irish inflections—was almost a species apart from Alfred and Colin.

"You fancy poetry, I trust, though you spurn the Bard?" We were striding through the Faerieland graveyard.

"Actually—"

He stood stock-still and declaimed:

And when convulsive throes denied my breath

The faintest utterance to my fading thought,

To thee—to thee—e'en in the grasp of death

My spirit turned, oh! oftener than it ought.

Thus much and more; and yet thou lov'st me not,

And never wilt! Love dwells not in our will.

Nor can I blame thee, though it be my lot

To strongly, wrongly, vainly, love thee still.

"Do you know who wrote that?"

"Shakespeare?" I ventured.

"Byron. How about this?" Again, he proceeded to recite:

> I knew a flower whose leaves were meant to bloom
> Till Death should snatch it to adorn the tomb,
> Now, blanching 'neath the blight of hopeless grief
> With never blooming and yet living leaf;
> A flower on which my mind would wish to shine,
> If but one beam could break from mind like mine:
> I had an ear which could on accents dwell
> That might as well say "perish" as "farewell!"
> An eye which saw, far off, a tender form
> Beaten, unsheltered, by affliction's storm:
> An arm—a lip—that trembled to embrace
> My Angel's gentle breast and sorrowing face,
> A mind that clung to Ouse's fertile side
> While tossing—objectless—on Menai's tide!

"Byron?" I conjectured.

"Thank you very much," he said, puffing out his chest. "The poet's name is Brontë, Patrick Branwell."

"That is *your* composition?"

"Indeed. And there are many others beside. I aim to be a poet and painter of portraits. Did I mention that *Coleridge* admired my work?"

I looked blank.

"Not Samuel Taylor, of course—he's been gone these ten long years. But his son, Hartley, encouraged me to translate Horace, which I did—the first volume of *Odes*, anyway. He was *greatly* impressed by my rhymes."

Reader, I confess that in those days, the name of Coleridge was yet unknown to me—fils, or père. Still, to my youthful ears, his artistic ambitions impressed.

"Whatever are you doing in Haworth?" I asked. I felt that after his disclosure, I was entitled to such a query.

"Oh, well ... I'm on leave, y'see—as tutor to the Robinsons' son. They're a *very* wealthy family at Thorp Green round York. Do you know them?"

"I fear not."

"Pity. They are practically royal. Dear Anne was governess to the girls, all sweet; and Mrs. Robinson, well—she is just this side of an Angel!"

I lifted my eyes toward Heaven. How many times in London had I heard this hackneyed phrase? Why were women always sainted and not allowed to be flesh?

Branwell's account had so absorbed me that I had neglected my role as spy. Above all things, I did not wish to disappoint Isabelle.

"Your sisters—do they ... do they write poems as well?"

"Never. We all wrote stories as children, but *I* am the one who will immortalize the name of Brontë!"

He thrust out his arms like an animate statue. His whole being vibrated with confidence—something I much admired—but felt a terrible dearth of myself.

I attempted to convey my support. "Indeed, I wish you all the luck. Father says that the Arts are tenuous, and not fit, for—how shall I say it?—"

"Rising personages such as yourself? And that is why, I own, you have been sent to Lake Leman, to Exile in Chillon!"

A double dungeon wall and wave
Have made—and like a living grave
Below the surface of the lake
The dark vault lies wherein we lay;
We heard it ripple night and day,
     Sounding o'er our heads it knock'd;
And I have felt the winter's spray
Wash through the bars when winds were high
And wanton in the happy sky;
     And then the very rock hath rock'd,
     And I have felt it shake, unshock'd,
Because I could have smiled to see
The death that would have set me free.

"Thank you," I responded. "That certainly makes me feel cheerful. May we cease all poetry for now? My head is ready to burst from a surfeit of heated lines."

"Of course. Shall we discuss more mundane matters?"

"Yes … 'Victoria and Adelaide'—are these perhaps Parsonage servants who reside out of doors?"

Branwell's wire glasses shook as he attempted not to laugh. "Hmmm … one might say that they are useful, but only upon a plate."

"Oh." I looked horrified.

"They are Emily's pet geese. They make their home in the peat house."

I blushed.

"There is also a hawk named Hero. Kindly do not mistake him for Prometheus, bound in the cellar."

I averted my head. "No."

I felt as if I could never succeed with these Brontës—for everything I said was proved either wrong or foolish. I determined on our walk back to discourse as little as possible.

"It is a beautiful day, is it not?" Branwell gestured to barren trees lining the two-sided graveyard.

"Mmmmm," I answered.

He gave me a rather strange look, then opened the door to the Parsonage.

"Did you enjoy your perambulation?" asked Anne. She was the only one left at table.

"Mmmmm."

"It seems the very effort has rendered her incapable of speech." Branwell shrugged before his sister, then clambered upstairs.

Anne gave me an alarmed glance and continued with her sewing. The grandfather clock on the landing ticked away the seconds languidly.

FIRST LESSONS: MISS EMILY

As it happened, Branwell departed that week to retake his place at Thorp Green. After saying his noisy good-byes, he slammed out of the Parsonage to make the four-mile walk to Keighley. In my unspoken opinion, these Brontës had missed their true calling: they should have been mountaineers.

After a fusillade of gunfire (to which I confess I was getting accustomed), I made my way down to breakfast, espying the solitary Anne. She seemed startled by my presence, as if I were an intruder. She solemnly bowed her head and mouthed a mealtime prayer.

"Miss Anne," I said at last, "are you not grieved that you do not accompany your brother?"

"Oh no," she replied with vigor. "You do not comprehend a governess's life. Your time is never your own, as you are expected to labor from dawn into the dark hours."

"Yet you are compensated for your work." As a member of the upper class, I felt annoyed by her complaint.

"Yes. Forty pounds a year. If one broke that into an hourly wage, it were better to toil in a mill." I perceived that when she spoke of matters of the heart, her shyness fell away.

"Indeed, I hope you may attract more pupils." This was not entirely selfless, for I wanted others to share in a portion of my misery. I dug into my porridge, recalling Father's table: not an inch of cloth could be seen under silver trays bursting with food. And the endless pourings of tea! I stared into my empty cup and sighed.

Anne must have received this as a sign of my impatience. "Today, Maria, begins your official term. You are to take lessons with Miss Emily. Please see her in back." She gestured toward the half-open kitchen door.

I raised an eyebrow. Was I to be taught in the province of servants? Perhaps I was expected to assist with the midday meal. Feeling highly aggrieved, I flounced through the door.

I found Emily standing at a table, actually *baking bread* while reading a propped-up tome in some foreign tongue. The black stove fire blazed as a brass kettle hung above it.

My instructor looked up briefly.

"You're late. Also, that is the most ridiculous costume I have ever seen. Impractical in every way."

My lower lip started to quiver, and hot liquid ran down my cheeks.

"None of that! Unlike male Professors, I am *not* susceptible to tears."

I wiped my eyes with the back of my hand.

"For God's sake, child, pull up a chair and sit down!"

I had rarely heard blasphemy before, and certainly not from a woman! Shocked, I sat, keeping my distance from this harsh mistress.

She continued her lecture. "Why prance around in petticoats in a harsh clime such as this? Who did you think to impress? Old Tabby?"

With Herculean effort, I managed to hold my tongue. Emily herself was dressed in the queerest manner: she sported the huge puffed sleeves, or "gigot," which had fallen out of fashion in the thirties; and her homemade dress hung, sans corset, all too close to her thin frame. What was more, flour splotched her front and she did not care to tidy herself. *How had this being survived in a posh capital like Brussels?*

"Let us commence. Are you versed in any language? "French, German, Italian?"

"I do speak French. A *very* little."

"*Crois-tu que tu es la jeune fille la plus ignorante que tu connais?*"[1]

"Um, *fille* . . ."

"*C'est vrais que tu as été renvoyé par six écoles différentes en raison d'être complètement idiote?*"[2]

This seemed to be a question, and my interrogator was clearly expecting an answer.

"*Oui,*" I replied.

"*Alors, c'est tout a fait une perte de temps d'essayer de t' apprendre quelque chose, n'est-ce pas?*"[3]

"*Oui, mademoiselle.*"

"Well, at least you are honest. And I thought my Law Hill pupils were the very model of insipidity."

Never in my life had I been spoken to in such a manner! I clenched my fists at my side, on the verge of a hot rebuttal.

Emily took no notice. She closed the book before her and pulled two others out from a cupboard. "We are going to start with Latin."

---

[1] "Would you say that you're the most ignorant young girl of your acquaintance?"

[2] "And that you've been expelled from six different schools for being a complete dunce?"

[3] "Therefore, trying to teach you anything is a complete waste of my time?"

"What? That is absurd! It is hardly the province of girls." This, along with her mocking manner, proved positively insufferable.

"It is the root of all Romance language. Learn this, and you will understand the others' etymology."

I had no idea what "en-ti-mol-gy" was. I glanced down at the well-worn volumes she handed me: one was a Latin grammar; the other had been penned by a person called Ovid.

"And you learned all this in Brussels?"

Her laugh was more like a snort. "Self-study, with considerable help from Anne. Papa taught her briefly."

This violated all my precepts. Classics were never meant for our sex—they were meant for Oxford and Cambridge! Nor should a well-bred young lady be exposed to Byron and Shakespeare. I had heard as much from half a dozen headmistresses, and shook my head in mute rebellion.

Emily was oblivious.

"I wish you to employ that grammar to translate a line—*a single line*—from Ovid. Let us see if that unplowed mind of yours can yield some fertile soil."

Reader, I confess I wanted to strangle her! It was more than apparent she had nothing but contempt for her pupils. Which brought me to this bold question:

"Miss Emily, if you despise the impartation of learning, why then become a teacher?"

"I am doing it for Charlotte," she said. "And Anne. This school scheme is dear to their hearts."

For the briefest of moments, I thought she might possess a soul. But this hope was dashed as she addressed me in some harsh alien tongue:

"Suche Zuflucht in Deiner strengen Pflicht!"[4]

---

[4] Let you betake yourself to your harsh duty!

This seemed to be a dismissal. I slunk out of the kitchen and bolted upstairs to my room. Throwing the books on my bed, I followed them with my own person.

The realization dawned on me then as to exactly where I was. Had I been able to express it, I should have said I had traveled from the kitchen fire — into the heart of Hell.

FIRST LETTER HOME

Haworth—Yorkshire
16 January 1844

Dearest Isabelle,

I beg your forgiveness for being remiss in writing, but as you might surmise, I have spent these first two weeks adjusting to my new environs.

Oh, Isabelle! What I wouldn't give to be back at 30—— Harley Street, surrounded by your sweet self and even the bothersome Emma. This place—this, this <u>Yorkshire</u>—is too horrid to be imagined! Not only is the temperature frigid but the denizens are either harsh workingmen or strange alien beings (the Brontës!) who seem to have dropped from the sky.

Can you fathom, Isabelle, that they actually expected I would <u>walk</u>—<u>in the falling snow!</u>—the four miles from Keighley? Such are the creatures I find here. Happily, the Parsonage itself has proved adequate. The food is modest but well prepared (seemingly by the sisters themselves) and the accommodations neat—but <u>the people, Isabelle, the people</u>!

I hardly know where to begin . . . I shall start with the dearly departed . . . there was a brother—a curious, exuberant chap with hair the color of henna. He was much given to spouting poesy—<u>in the middle of a graveyard</u>.

The father is a stern old clergyman who sits by himself for the most part: he is much a creature of habit, winding the grandfather clock each night at nine o'clock <u>precisely</u>. I would hardly disturb your delicate mind with reports of gunshot, but yes, this is a daily ritual, as sure as the crowing of the cock!

As for the three sisters about whom you were curious—to me they are matched in learning but wholly dissimilar in temperament. The eldest Miss Brontë has moods which seemingly depend on the post: whenever she sends a letter, she is in high spirits (and far higher when she <u>receives</u> one), but—if too much time passes ere a reply, she plunges into a temper just this side of Bedlam. I tell you frankly, Isabelle, I believe her to be half mad.

The youngest, Anne, is the most comely in person: she has lovely blue eyes, and a fairish complexion that reminds me of myself. She is quite demure and, I take it, highly devout, for she is often at prayer.

<u>But the median Miss Brontë</u>! Oh sweet Isabelle, she is a horror straight from a Gothic (not that I've ever read one, but I can only conjecture). She dresses with a complete disregard for fashion, and every word she lets fall is laced with mockery and insult.

This "Miss Emily" is an oddity who best belongs under glass. There is no weather she will not walk in; and I have sometimes come upon her when she is lost in a sort of trance—*mumbling to herself.*

In light of all these particulars, I <u>beg you,</u> dear Isabelle, to work upon Father daily until he releases me from this burden! I feel much like an inmate, condemned to spend her ebbing days in the dungeons of Che-lon! By the waters of Lake L-something.

If you truly love me—if you are indeed my closest friend—please expend every effort to free me from this personal H——!

Love,
Your Dearest Friend Maria

P.S: Please send warmest regards to Messrs. Colin and Alfred.

LESSON 2: MISS EMILY

How I loathed my coming audience with the dread Miss Emily! When I crept downstairs for tea, I found both Charlotte and Anne. They motioned me to sit, and we began our modest repast. I tried as hard as I might to stifle thoughts of sponge cakes and sandwiches; fresh-baked scones and cream; capped by a selection of *five* India teas. I sighed as I picked up my cup.

Charlotte appeared to be in one of her better moods. She clasped a letter in her hand, reading eagerly as she ate. Anne, however, was glum and pale. She broached what I considered a peculiar teatime topic.

"Oftentimes I miss Aunt," she sighed.

"As do I. After all, it was her largesse that enabled our trip to Belgium."

Do you not believe what she said of the Calvinists? What if they are correct?"

"Dear Anne, we have walked this moribund field so often. Do not oppress your spirit—recall how ill it once made you."

"Yes." Anne bent her head. "But what if Aunt was right and only the Elect are saved? What then of the sinful man—will her ever earn God's grace?"

"I cannot speak for our Maker, but I do know of whom you speak." Charlotte gave me a guarded glance. "He is grown, he is independent of you now, and he will do—or not—exactly as he pleases. Recall that heeding the advice of others has never been a salient suit." Now she looked angry. "Let us do what we can in our own sphere and conscience. As for others, persuasion is as foolish as trying to catch the moon."

Anne nodded, but did not seem assuaged.

"Ah, Maria." Charlotte suddenly addressed me. "I was distracted by my sister. Miss Emily would like to see you, to discover the fruits of this morning's lesson."

"More like worms," I muttered.

"She is to be found in the kitchen."

Naturally.

I ran upstairs to retrieve my books and a crossed-out mess of translation. With bowed head, I reemerged, went downstairs, and opened the kitchen door: for me, it might as well have been the Gates of Hell.

She was there, scribbling furiously in a notebook. Her work must have amused her, for she gave a delighted laugh. As she caught sight of my person, she snapped it shut.

"By the bye, since you have *not* bothered to inquire after the steed you stole from the carriage man, be assured he is well looked after at the Black Bull stable."

"What? Oh yes." In truth, amid my own troubles, Balthazar had completely slipped my mind.

"Well? How goes the labor of love with Ovid?"

"It is a labor, to be sure." I produced my disgraceful sheet.

"Hmmm. You have translated *Est deus in nobis,* 'There is a god within us,' as 'God sees all.'"

"Ummm . . ." I could feel the heat of contempt as surely as that of the stove. "Well, God *does* see all. Does He not?"

"Whether He does or even exists is not the matter at hand. You attempted to translate four simple words and have emerged with nonsense. Why you are even here is a riddle deeper than the Sphinx's."

That was the tipping point. My rage acted as a powerful spur to courage. "Have you no regard for the feelings of others?" I cried.

"Not yours," she answered easily. "In fact, I have more esteem for Keeper"—she pointed to her mastiff, who snoozed before the fire, head on enormous paws—"than I do for you. Come."

I felt tears sting my eyes as Emily strode from the room. Taking two steps for her every one, I trailed her into the study. Happily, Mr. Brontë was from home. Emily plunked herself on a stool at the pianoforte, sitting ramrod-straight before a pleated silk screen. With no musical sheets, she arched her long fingers and touched the ivory keys. I must confess I never heard such music in my life, not even in London. It rose, it enchanted, it diffused through the Parsonage and became a living entity. It poured into the study fire as if from a pot of gold. As her final note receded, the ensuing silence was mournful.

"Handel," she said, nonchalantly. "Do you play?" Still under the spell of her genius, I stepped to the side of the instrument.

"No, Miss. Not even a little." There was hardly a point in deceiving this prodigy. Although I loved music, I was as dreadful attempting to produce it as she herself was proficient.

Emily vacated her perch, pointing for me to take her place. As if I could, or would ever be able to! I plunked out some childish melody—made unrecognizable by all the sour notes—then halted in frustration.

"It appears that Mr. Chopin need not trouble himself."

I looked down.

"Let me give you some basic exercises."

She did, and I managed at once to create a fretful dissonance. I saw her flounce onto a sofa in the dining room, placing small balls of rolled-up yarn in her ears. Keeper began to yowl, and I could see from my seat that she did all she could to encourage him.

Truly, at that moment, I would have been overjoyed if the floor had opened beneath her, showering her with sulphur and hellfire.

SECOND LETTER HOME

Haworth—Yorkshire
17 January 1844

Dearest Father,

~~I am desperate.~~ First, allow me to inquire as to your health and that of my siblings. I trust you are all making merry while I sink into despair.

Oh Sir, the situation I find myself in is the <u>worst</u> of my young life! What I would not give now for fifty Miss M——'s, even with her scoldings and musty ancient scent.

Father, these infernal Misses Brontë do their best to mete out torture on an almost <u>hourly</u> basis! Do you know they are teaching me <u>Latin</u>, to be followed by geography? Upon my return, I shall be unfit to assume the mantle of Wife.

As for the Parsonage environs, it is one of genteel poverty. Not only do the sisters sew their own clothes but actually <u>reuse paper</u>—writing crosshatched so as to preserve the precious sheets.

I am sure Isabelle has informed you about declaiming Shakespeare at table. Even the youngest, and most pious, is guilty of admiring Cowper, a person or persons called Coleridge, and—dare I say it?—Lord Byron! There—you see I am coarsened already.

Please Sir, cease this unfeeling campaign and send me wherever you please. Even darkest Chelon! I await your response with trembling heart, for I do not think I can endure longer. Certainly not more than a day.

Love,
Your Eldest (and Most <u>Obedient</u> Daughter),
Maria Victoria

P S.: Would you kindly send some chocolates along with your reply?

FIRST LESSON: MISS ANNE

It was not until my third week's residence that I partook of lessons from anyone but Emily. I continued my assault on Latin and a worse one on music. I attempted to play a tune without setting Keeper to howling. I could have sworn that one afternoon, I saw him cover his ears with his paws. Anne's sweet spaniel, Flossy, seemed nonplussed by the din.

Poor Martha Brown, the young girl who aided Tabby, had her own burdens. She had taken to wearing earmuffs as she went about her chores—*inside* the Parsonage. It seemed every moment I spent there was redolent with insult.

When Anne first called me into the dining room (which served as the sister's study), I did not feel the same dread as when Emily summoned. Though it would be strange to be taught with no potatoes present, I determined to make the attempt.

"Please—take a seat." Anne's demeanor was mild as always, but she had the stern air of experience and would clearly brook no dissent.

"We begin with the science of geography. Can you tell me in what continent the Ural Mountains reside?"

"Well, not England." It was a semi-educated guess in light of the country's general flatness.

"Does 'Ural' sound like an English word?"

"No. Rather . . . German?"

"The Ural Mountains are in Russia and form the boundary of Europe and Asia."

"Oh."

"Where are the Alps?"

"Switzerland!" I cried. Father had made many a visit.

"Also Italy, France, Germany, and Austria. Where are *we*, Miss Maria?"

"Yorkshire!" This I was sure I got right.

"And our nearest mountains?"

I thought. "The Downs?"

"The Pennines. Which part of Britain lies just to the north of us?"

"Ireland?"

Poor Anne. She put a hand to her head. "Miss Maria, I was governess for nearly four years to the two young Robinson girls. Yet I must observe, though it grieves me, that you are more ignorant than the both of them put together."

This harsh judgment took me aback. My cheeks hot, I stood abruptly.

"I had not thought *you*, Miss Anne, to be cruel as your sister! If you will excuse me." I turned, preparing to flounce upstairs.

"Miss Maria." Anne's quiet voice nevertheless shook me. "I must inform you that once, at the Ingham's, I tied my pupils to a table leg to keep them at their lessons."

I froze, looking back. Though Anne presented herself as meek, I sensed she possessed a steel spine. She *had* to, to survive so long as a governess. Putting my pique aside, I retook my place at the table.

"Let us move to arithmetic," she said coolly. "Tell me, what is six plus eight?"

"Fifteen."

"And twenty less five and a half?"

"Twelve."

"Are you *guessing* the answers?"

"Yes, Miss Anne."

"What is your experience in this discipline?"

"Poor. Very poor."

"Poor instruction or poor attention?"

"Well, I should say one-fourth the former and three-fourths the latter."

Anne laughed in a way that distinguished her from Emily: she made you feel that *you* were not her jest's object. "That is the best usage of sums you have so far displayed."

I smiled. This was the first actual *compliment* I had so far received at the school.

"I am going to give you a book." She pulled out a thinnish volume. I saw it to be a simple text on mathematics, perhaps geared to very young boys.

"Inside, you will find the tables of arithmetic. At first, they might seem tedious, since they must be memorized, but once you have mastered them, you will be ready for problem solving. And that part I think you'll enjoy."

Her pleasant expression and warmth convinced me that she was genuine. I gratefully accepted the primer.

"Do you like to draw?" she inquired, hefting a heavy portfolio onto the table.

I sighed. "It is entirely possible I am a worse artist than musician."

"As with all the arts, one must practice diligently."

She pulled out a detailed pencil sketch of a bridge with a lone figure atop. The trees surrounding its water-filled tunnels were wondrously lifelike, while the faint image of a church hung ghostlike at the horizon. Truly, this was a fine piece: as fine as any I had seen.

I shook my head slowly. "Miss Anne, it seems that you and your family are *so* very talented. Your brother is a poet, Miss Emily is a prodigy, *you* are a superb artist, and I expect that Miss Brontë has some gift of her own."

Anne faced me with a half smile.

"I find it truly astonishing that a family confined to a—forgive me if I say 'remote village'—exhibits such mastery."

"I thank you, Miss Maria. God bestows His gifts where He may. Now let us have *you* attempt a drawing."

As with Emily, I felt the harsh pull of dread. I approached a blank sheet of paper, wielding a shaky pencil. I thought to depict Keeper's head, since an animal sketch must be easy. Alas, not for *me.* Anne took up my shoddy work, which appeared to be that of a goblin with a giant, lolling tongue.

"Interesting," she remarked, though she probably wanted to flee. "Perhaps if I guided your hand . . ."

She stood directly behind me and seized the writing implement as she directed my wrist. Before I knew it, I saw the face of a handsome young man before me.

"Bravo!" I cried. I decided to tease her a little. "Is this the visage of an acquaintance? Someone perhaps who admires you?"

She stiffened like a block of marble, turning to that stone's pale shade. I could not understand. All of my other teachers—old maids every one—had *welcomed* talk of suitors, most of them imagined. What could have possibly prompted such an extreme reaction from Anne?

"That will be all for today. I expect you to practice your sums and sketches, and show a glimmer of progress when we meet tomorrow. Start by tracing pictures in books."

She turned about gracefully, mounted the stairs, and was gone.

I again studied the likeness that had turned her cold: a fair young man in his twenties, with blue eyes and curly dark hair swept dramatically toward his temple.

All evening until bedtime, I attempted to memorize sums. Yet my mind continued to drift toward a more intriguing topic: *Who was the man in the picture? And did he admire her still?*

RESPONSE FROM HOME – 1

At long last, I received a letter. I had seen Charlotte accept what seemed like a handful each day, but this was the first time an envelope—sloppily addressed, to be sure—had been handed by Martha to me.

Clutching my treasure to my breast (as I had seen Charlotte do often), I retreated up to my room to read the precious missive. I saw at once that it was from Isabelle:

London
?? January 1844

My Dearest Dearest Friend,

How low I became upon reading your pathetic lines! Truly, your bondage in that G–dforsaken place rivals that of the ancient Hebrews. I am <u>so, so</u> sorry, Maria, that your sojourn among the savages is even worse than what we imagined while you were still cradled in the bosom of London.

<u>Perhaps this news will cheer you</u>: I am attending the Whittome's ball tonight, and shall be wearing a blue silk gown—<u>how</u> you would covet it! At the Almacks' Ball last Wednesday, my card was overflowing ere I stepped into the rooms. I was much admired (of course), but have decided

to set my hat on <u>the eldest son of a Duke</u>! I do believe he noticed my presence, for he delivered a wink as I waltzed past with a lesser partner.

Tomorrow, we embark to Her Majesty's to hear some boring opera, but I remain unperturbed. Shall I wear my embroidered pink muslin or the solemn grey satin?—so many choices lie before me!

Emma, George, and I attended a play at the Haymarket, then heard a Mr. Frank List (or some foreigner or other) at the pianoforte. The season is <u>at its height</u> here, and we are preparing to depart for Briarwood once our engagements conclude. The weather has generally been mild and clear— so different from the polar drifts which you describe with such feeling!

Alas—must dash now, dearest—~~Sir Shelby is bellowing from downstairs~~! Love and kisses from George and Emma; <u>we all think of you daily</u>!

Your,

Isabelle

Well. Once I would have been ravenous to devour news of Society, but now, I was not quite sure how to digest this meal. Of course, I longed to attend the events that Isabelle limned with such fever; but a new, contrary flavor rose to sour my palette: some might call it Distaste.

Balls, opera, finery: what use were they to me now? I lived amongst a people who spurned such pleasures— who clung almost like Quakers to their plain manner of living. Undoubtedly, this stemmed from poverty—from the pinched constraints of living on a clergyman's salary—and from the sermons preached each Sunday at Mr. Brontë's pulpit.

For one of the first times in my life, I found myself confused: drawn to the glittery rooms of London and at the same time ... repelled by them. I could not understand my own Self, which heretofore had comprised a girl of few—but extravagant—tastes.

There was also a shade of something in the tone of Isabelle's letter: a sort of willful joie de vivre that dwelt solely on its own pleasure. Did my friend *truly* bemoan my absence? Or was I but a bit of gossip between Vauxhall and Covent Garden?

Contrary notions of mind were not at that time my strong suit. I found my head swimming and on the verge of headache. Had they not been so socially backward, I might have consulted the Brontës, for I knew they possessed good sense. Yet what could *they* know of high life—the doings of their betters, even of the titled? I laughed aloud at the thought of Charlotte—distressingly small and plain—even aware of such a milieu. Possessed by this good humor, I made my way downstairs, hoping to find some amusement.

A SPECTRAL PRESENCE

I found the lower floor as good as uninhabited. Mr. Brontë was locked in his study, and frankly, that was my preference. There was no question he was lively, what with his morning pistol, dislike of all Dissenters, and shockingly liberal politics. He told me he had actually voted *for* the Catholic Emancipation Bill! In my ignorance then, thought: *What could you expect from an Irishman?* (Though this particular one possessed a Cambridge degree.)

In accord with Irish Rebellion, Charlotte was at this moment stomping across her floorboards, and I heard the distinct sound of an object being smashed. Anne had disappeared into some quiet corner, and Emily—well!— no doubt she was striding the moors, thumbing her nose at the god of Winter.

That afternoon, I frankly gave thanks to be alone. From the dining room table, I picked up my chewed pencil, ready to trace a picture from an enormous book—which involved a bird called Audubon—when I spied something intriguing.

A small door beneath the staircase's half landing had been left slightly ajar. I must confess, I had never noted this entrance previously. In the waning light of the northern sky, I could just make out the silhouette of a roughhewn step.

In my own spirit of rebellion, I crept silently forward. After surveying the hall to insure the absence of Tabby and Martha, I placed a slippered foot on that first stone block. Gazing down into the murk, I could sight only odd-shaped piles whose contents remained unknown.

Seized by a sharp curiosity, I crept down the curved staircase, to find myself in . . . a rather nondescript cellar. I confess I felt somewhat deflated. Owing to the Gothic nature of the Parsonage (and certainly of its inmates!), I half expected to encounter a corpse, or at least a living phantom. Alas, the only object in view was a small fermenter that smelled vaguely of beer. So much for my thrilling adventure.

I turned to remount the stairs, coughing away some elder cobwebs. Yet just as I did so, I heard the sharp report of a foot; I spotted movement—yes! *Something* was floating beneath the vaulted ceiling, and I could swear— it was unmistakable now—that what accosted me in the darkness was the thin figure of a NUN!

She was clothed in black and white, but the ghastly aspect that horrified was . . . her face was all obscured, save for glinting dark eyes. No other feature protruded from that bandaged death mask!

I screamed my way up the staircase like the most deranged inmate at Bedlam. Mr. Brontë emerged from his study, a smoking pipe in one hand; Charlotte came as fast as she could, her neat waisted skirt swinging bell-like as she made her way to his side.

"Sacred Heaven! What ails you, Maria?" I observed that her skin was mottled and her dark eyes rimmed with red.

"I . . . I saw something. In the cellar." It required all of my will to prevent myself from trembling.

"Indeed?" Mr. Brontë seemed amused.

"What business had you there?" Charlotte placed her small hands on her hips.

"I—I was just exploring, when I saw it."

"What?" The two Brontës asked.

"It was—a supernal nun!" I felt like the worst kind of imbecile as the d— —ning words left my mouth.

"In a *Church of England* parsonage?" Mr. Brontë's immense cravat barely moved with his head.

"In a *Protestant* country where Papists have been reduced—thankfully—to a decided minority?"

Charlotte spat out the word "Papists." I had not known many myself, yet it was clear from the speaker's demeanor that she truly hated Catholics.

"Mayhap this poor garrl (as Mr. Brontë pronounced it) has been too much about har studies. She needs to get out—and these Romanist ghosts will trouble har no more."

Both Brontës waged a valiant struggle to rein in their laughter. Had there been a cellar door underneath the place where I stood, I wished it would have opened quickly to remove me from their sight.

Along with the smell of tobacco, Mr. Brontë returned to his study. Charlotte remounted the stairs. I looked out from a double-paned window. The earth was a vast snowball whose very air threatened to crack from its burden of heavy frost. No, I could not go out. I was a wretched captive, held by faerie folk who drew into their circle an avenger from the Old Church! Wracked by shock and despair, I rested my head upon cold glass and quietly sobbed aloud.

LETTERS TO AND FROM HOME

In the Afternoon of the Nun, Martha handed me another letter. This one was assuredly *not* from Isabelle, for I recognized Father's firm script.

30— — Harley Street
London

Maria,

Greatly troubled to learn of your difficulties abroad. However, I have received a note from Miss Brontë recounting your "considerable progress." The sisters are of a mind that you have some Promise lurking within. If so, this is a miracle just short of the Resurrection. <u>Under no circumstances</u> do I sanction a return from Haworth.
Try to insure that your next missive is considerably more cheerful.

Your Father,

Sir John Shelby

(P.S. I have eaten all the Belgian chocolates.)

"No!" I yelled into vacancy, taking up my pad and wounded pencil. Furiously, I began to scribble.

~~Father~~ Dear Father:

"Distress" is too inadequate a word to enumerate my feelings upon receipt of your letter. Indeed, you might as well have consigned me to the uneven tombs that grace the Parsonage's "garden."

But there is an urgent matter that must be imparted without delay. While wandering the household cellar earlier, I found myself assaulted by <u>a spectral presence</u>. Either this family of Brontë attracts visitors from Beyond (which frankly would not surprise me) or I myself am losing all reason and must be locked up straightaway!

Whichever be true, Sir, surely you can accede to my present removal. I must make haste—I hear the front door opening!—it is the <u>lunatic Emily</u>, fresh from a stroll among the icicles.

Begging You, Sir, To Relieve Me Of Present Distress,
I Remain,
Your Own Maria V. Shelby

THE ELDEST MISS BRONTË

February passed in a frigid haze of learning: tracing pictures with Anne; having my stubborn fingers seized and pinched by Emily; and even an examination—in geography. I cannot fail to report that I performed dismally.

On one unremarkable morning in March, Miss Brontë decided to take up her post and summoned me into her study. I had not associated much with her—save for the sorry scene of the Nun—but allow me to state, Reader: there was something in her mien that frightened me.

I felt, in some respects, that she was actually wilder than Emily, though outwardly more composed. The sparks emitted by her dark eyes, her varying moods, and frequent illness: all combined to make me think her slightly mad.

She turned those large eyes on me then. "Miss Emily informs me that your French is execrable."

"*Oui, Madamoiselle.*"

"And how are you at writing?"

"My hand is legible enough."

She turned in a kind of pain. "*Writing,* as in composing, devoirs, stories—"

"*Trop terrible!*" I replied. You see, Reader, I *had* been learning a little.

She sighed. "Let us kill the proverbial two birds with— I assume you can complete the phrase."

"One stone!" I crowed.

"Good. It heartens me to know that you possess at least folk knowledge." She drew herself up. "My mandate in this Establishment is to teach you the French language in the same manner as my beloved Professor." She paused, then seemed to gather herself. "M. Constantin Heger."

It might have been my youthful fancy, but I thought it cost her greatly merely to utter that name. I knew from Emily that she viewed him with contempt: she had told me, in the kitchen, that Heger had taught her *nothing*. Yet Charlotte just as surely made of him an idol.

"Here is a work I much value, written in French by M. George Sand."

I must have looked somewhat blank.

"In point of fact, M. Sand is a woman. She dresses in male costume, but that does not affect her artistry, which is of the highest order."

Inwardly, I groaned. Of course the peculiar Charlotte admired this freak of a foreigner!

"Here is today's lesson: Using the Heger method, read this book with the aid of a dictionary, but do *not* fixate on grammar. I wish you to capture the spine—the *essence*—of the work and compose a brief devoir—*in French*—paraphrasing same. *Comprenez-vous?*"

There were two possible responses, so I gave the one that sounded more positive. "*Oui.*"

"*Alors, si tu peux apprendre en utilisant la méthode d'Heger, tu as les potentialités d'être un vrai maître de littérature.*"[5]

---

[5] "If you can learn by the Heger Method, you have the potential of being a True Master of Literature."

She seemed to take a certain strength from conversing in that language, but the only words I recognized were "Heger" and "literature."

How I struggled with Sand's *Mauprat*! After all my lessons with Emily, I could barely say "hello" in French. I decided to focus on a passage making use of the word *"amour."* It was so *so* tedious, but my interest was piqued by the story. It was scandalous, to be sure, yet the romance thoroughly ensnared me, even in this alien tongue. I worked as hard as I could until the afternoon light grew dim.

Charlotte had gone out, leaving me alone to my task. At last, she returned with a clutch of envelopes in her gloves.

"No response. *Nothing.* It has been nearly two months." She said this in her natural voice, as if I were incorporeal. "I believe I discern the reason: the Inspector of Police sees all!"

I raised both of my brows: was it possible this demure woman was guilty of criminality?

She grabbed some sheets and an implement, pulled a chair close to the table, and proceeded to scribble furiously. I could almost *feel* the heat reflect from the metal tip of her pen. She dipped it so vehemently—and repeatedly—into a jar of ink that I feared she would soil her garment.

She looked, eyes afire, at me, who looked at her. "No staring, Miss Maria! Recommence your exercise." Under thrall to her emotions, she sounded more Irish than ever. I prayed she would not forget herself and lapse into incomprehensibility.

We sat thus for a half hour more, myself engrossed in a "naughty" French novel, and she composing a screed seemingly set at the same high pitch. We were interrupted at last by Emily's call from the kitchen.

"Charlotte, do your part and peel a potato!"

Her sister sighed, resting her pen in the ink and tucking her now-blackened sheets into the leaves of a book. She was so depleted by her efforts that she barely had the strength to walk the ten steps to the door.

Reader, by now you surely know my character as it was then. I was young, I was ignorant, and had not a mother to guide me. To put it another way, my respect for Privacy fell second to native Curiosity.

Like a thief from *Arabian Nights*, I tiptoed toward Charlotte's book, withdrew the deeply scratched sheets, and began to read. D——! *The entire thing was in French!* I dragged over my thick dictionary for another round of translation. This time, it was not Sand's effusions, but equally gripping prose that caused my pen to fly.

Haworth-Bradford-Yorkshire
4 March, 1844

Monsieur:

> Near two months have passed in which I have not received a reply. "Perhaps it was lost in the post," I told myself resignedly. But when no reply came to my second letter ... I realized that Monsieur is perhaps too busy to respond to his old friend and pupil ...
>
> <u>Yet I pray that this not be so</u>! Without the occasional missive from Monsieur—even your stern admonitions!—I do not know how I should find the strength to live! Our hamlet is so forlorn that we have attracted a single pupil to our newly formed Establishment. Never before have I been in

such dire want of Monsieur's advice. If my Master withdraws the light of his friendship, he plunges me into the darkest recess. And I cannot think, Monsieur, that this would be your desire!

Oh Monsieur, how sadly we parted! And with such haste and carelessness! I did not have the chance to tell you how much you mean to me—how I miss our literary exchanges, our English lessons, and your pronunciation of "Williams Shakspire"—even the pungent fragrance of your ever-present cigar!

Forgive my ramblings, Master. I am but a desolate being separated so far from you! I long for the day when I can return to Brussels, and then I shall see you again—indeed, it must be so—if not,

This was as far as *her* pen had sped.

Sweet Mother of Jesus! Yes, Reader, I—of bluest Shelby blood—was so rankled by what I read that I blasphemed in my mind. I hastily returned the sheets to their book, shoved my own into the fire, and retook my place by George Sand.

Yet the Frenchwoman's prose was *nothing* compared to Charlotte Brontë's! My God, what lake of fire seethed in that woman's heart, beneath those prim collars and colorless frocks? Unable to keep my seat, I began pacing around the table.

There was no doubt—*how could there be?*—that Charlotte adored Monsieur. Also no doubt—and I had heard this from Emily, who could as soon lie as dance a waltz at Saint James—that Monsieur had a wife—*there lived a Mme. Heger!*—and what was more fantastic: *a brood of six small children!*

To my prurient mind, it was delightfully immoral. I realized—even at my age—that Charlotte did not write her Master for "friendship" or advice. No! *She loved him*—loved him as passionately as a woman ever loved a man. I felt a shiver run through me. *I* had never been captive to such a feeling: as if I would die if I could not glimpse my beloved.

And what of *his* cruel silence, adding abject suffering to her insulated days? Yet I also asked myself: how *could* he address such letters without compromise to himself, the writer, and even his own wife? Please God that Madame knew nothing, for had she read Charlotte's effusions, surely she would do all to prevent their furtherance.

Who else knew of this fever? I discarded Mr. Brontë and Anne—they would have been shocked to their devout cores. *Emily?* She was so above human affairs that she could probably keep a secret, but what would her judgment be? She clearly disliked the object—and knowing her—would dismiss her sister's feelings, most likely as contemptible weakness.

What about those beyond the family sphere? Had Charlotte unburdened her heart to her two great correspondents: Ellen Nussey and Mary Taylor? Or would these two daughters of the clergy swoon if they knew of her declarations? *Especially to a foreigner, a probable Catholic, and the married father of six!*

My heart beat with rapidity. I grasped the back of Emily's chair. How could such a matter ever be resolved? And the largest question of all, one that overhung the Parsonage like a swirling curtain: what were *Monsieur's* feelings? To him, was Charlotte just another English schoolgirl or the woman he loved beyond measure but could never make his own?

Reader, I actually felt faint. A thrill ran through my body, setting my hairs on end!

Gradually, I returned to earth. I could smell comforting odors wafting in from the kitchen. I glanced down at *Mauprat*. Poor Madame Sand had been forgotten. Mere *tales* of Romance could no longer hold me, not with a *real one*—big as the Pennines!—on the brink of avalanche and threatening to engulf us.

Despite my better instincts, I gave a contented smile. Perhaps this Yorkshire outpost would prove interesting after all.

ATTEMPTING TO FIND OUT

Reader, as you might conjecture, after my Great Finding—as significant to me as the discovery of the Pyramids—schoolwork became secondary to my new occupation: attempting to find out exactly *what* had transpired in Brussels.

My first subject was Anne. A poor choice, I know, but she was my morning instructor.

"And what is seven times five?"

"Thirty-five," I answered. All that rote work appeared to be yielding results.

"Excellent. And twelve plus seventeen?"

"Twenty-nine. Miss Anne, may I ask you a question?"

"Of course." She turned to me with her mild blue eyes.

"Why was it that you remained at home when your sisters journeyed to Brussels?"

She nodded. "It was purely pecuniary. When Aunt Branwell died, she left a sum sufficient to send two of us abroad."

"I see. Does anyone keep in touch—with Brussels, that is?"

"Not to my certain knowledge. M. Heger was kind enough to grant Miss Brontë a certificate from the Athénée Royal. That was in December, and I believe the last point of contact. If we may proceed to long division—"

Ha! Just as I had surmised: Anne was wholly ignorant of the storm raging around her. Despite my better instincts, I next approached Emily.

"Stop that infernal racket!"

I was seated at the pianoforte, doing my best not to massacre some sonata by Beethoven. Emily put a hand to her forehead in despair.

"Miss Emily—" I strove to swing the discourse back to my favorite subject. "Forgive me, but I am curious. Did you teach music while in Brussels?"

Her tall frame bent over me. "I did."

"And how did you find your students?"

"Abysmal. Worse even than you."

I quelled my desire to kick her and assumed a tone of innocence. "Did M. Heger oversee your lessons?"

"That histrionic buffoon! He should have been on the stage."

"Indeed?"

"He would bellow and rage until he made the girls cry, then assuage them with smiles. The consummate 'French' raconteur."

I was unsure of the advisability of continuing. Emily seemed to me fully capable of violence. Still, I plunged on.

"In your opinion, is it possible that some of the girls might have fallen in love with him?"

She snorted. "Undoubtedly. The weakness of unformed minds."

I leaped. "Was he handsome then?"

"Who?" She reengaged herself with my world.

"M. Heger."

"Oh, he was little and dark. Always dressed in black. I have heard Charlotte—Miss Brontë—describe him as 'a black and sallow tiger.'"

"Did he have a particular favorite?"

She stared at me.

"Among the pupils, I mean."

"None that I could discern. Now let us cease this nonsensical prattle and return to 'Für Elise.'"

Well. My efforts had at least gained me a lingering mental picture. With caution, I next decided to consult the source.

That afternoon, Charlotte and I were in her study, reviewing my work on *Mauprat.* She nodded as she perused my devoir.

"Yes. You have captured the feel of the story and thrown grammar to the winds. Later, technical finesse will come."

"Merci, Mademoiselle."

"You have a true sensibility for the love of Bernard and Edmée."

I determined to seize the day. "Yes, Miss. I find it all so terribly sad: here are a man and woman perfectly suited to each other, yet at first he is so ignorant, and she so very schooled. Then he does not understand that she loves him and goes off for years. So tragic, do you not agree—an unrequited love of that kind?"

"Indeed, you have a profound understanding." Charlotte looked down and neatly folded her hands. "But yes, I should say the circumstances lead to extreme sadness. Be aware, however, that life offers far worse. Deeper than melancholy lies heartbreak."

I shot her a guarded glance. I could see her biting her lip, resisting a stubborn film of liquid pooling behind her glasses. Even I, in my investigative zeal, could not be so heartless as to continue my line of inquiry.

"I fear you are ill, Miss Brontë. I shall leave you to recuperate."

As it was still near freezing, I slipped into my warmest wool, wrapped a scarf about my throat, strapped on mittens and a muff, and stepped out on what was— beneath billows of snow—undoubtedly manicured lawn.

The cold assaulted my every pore—even through layers of petticoats—and I walked as fast as I could, thinking to visit my poor old horse down by the Black Bull.

As I struggled downhill, I experienced something wholly foreign. For the first time in my life, I actually felt pity for a being other than myself. The sensation was not unwelcome as I attempted to cogitate: How could *I* help Miss Brontë? How could *I* be the instrument so she could somehow shake off her Great Love or—in some yet-to-be revealed manner—attain it?

My mind was thus engaged as I sought to deter death at the hands of Main Street's cobblestones.

DISMISSED (AGAIN)

I left the Old White Lion Inn behind, where Martha's sister had employment, making my way past shops to the squarish, dark-bricked Black Bull, which emitted smoke from its single chimney. I hastened around to the stable to find Balthazar standing quietly, munching a mouthful of hay. Overcome with guilt for my neglect, I withdrew an apple abducted from Tabby and offered it on my palm. He inhaled the fruit in a single bite, pushing forward for more.

"No no, big man," I chided. "I shall bring you carrots on my next visit." I patted his giant muzzle, positioned on a face fully ten times the size of mine. I gave his thick neck a pat and breathed in the familiar scent of horse.

My sense of comfort was dashed as the back door to the tavern slammed open, and a staggering, laughing figure fell headfirst into the snow. Two companions—equally unsteady—lifted him by his arms and set him on the general road. As I glanced guardedly at the inebriate's face, I saw that I knew him, recognizing the aquiline nose and short, straggly beard.

"Branwell!" I cried, rushing from Balthazar's stall and forgoing all formality, so shocked was I to see him.

"Well now, it's Missy Miss, is it?" He squinted through frosted glasses.

I stiffened. "Miss Maria, I thank you."

"Fine, all right." He actually stumbled *uphill*.

I adopted my usual manner. "What brings you here, Mr. Brontë? It was my understanding that you are engaged at the Robinsons' at least until Easter week."

"Robinson, Robinson, oh! How she looked at my expulsion!" He pulled a small flask from under his coat, taking a few hasty gulps.

"Do you not think you have imbibed sufficient?" I tried to be as frigid as the white drifts we slogged through.

"Never sufficient, never." He actually started to sob. I had never been exposed to a man making such an exhibit, and so walked in silence beside him.

"She doesn't love him, *no!* She loves me—didn't she say so?"

"I shall not be so impertinent as to question the identity of 'she.'"

"Mrs. Robinson, of course—dear Lydia! Her husband has sent me out—oh God, I wish I were dead!"

"Compose yourself," I said coolly. "Do you wish to make a public scene? At the least, think of your sisters."

My words seemed to have an effect. Branwell wiped his eyes and almost managed to walk without stumbling.

I was unable to mask my irritation. "What is it with you Brontës? Are you wholly consumed by your passions?"

"Beg pard—?" Branwell slurred. "Or should that be, *'Oro ueniam'?*"

"A true gentleman holds his liquor," I lectured, feeling utter disgust. I thought of Alfred and Colin, never brighter than after a third glass of wine.

"Did I say I was true?" he shouted. *"Or a gentleman?"*

"Shhhh! The whole of Haworth will hear you!"

"Let them. Let them know that for *the third time,* I have been dismissed."

"From Thorp Green?" I did not quite comprehend.

"Ha! First from the Postlethwaites; then from Luddenden Foot, and now from the Robinsons. It appears, Missy Miss, that I 'canna' retain a post."

His laugh was so unnatural that I sought to distract him.

"And what sort of work have you done?"

This seemed to inspire loquaciousness.

"I was tutor to the Postlethwaites, but alas, sacked for drunkenness. Then I was clerk at the railroad, but eleven pounds, 1 shilling, and 7 pence went missing—*I* did not take it, but still. And as you are aware, lately I've been tutor to Edmund. Now what to do? I shall never see *her* again!"

He nearly fell over a snowdrift. I grabbed his tight upper sleeve, setting his human ship aright.

"Hear me." I sought to be stern. "When you enter the Parsonage, try to be pleasant to your sisters. Is Anne aware of your plight?"

"No, but she will know the reason."

"Indeed. She is quiet but hardly a fool."

"I fear dear Charlotte's wrath!"

"I very much doubt she has cause to chastise *you*."

He looked at me with vacancy. So he too was in the shadows. Unlike the loose-tongued Shelbys, these Brontës could keep a secret—mayhap to the grave and beyond.

We walked a short distance uphill, garnering stares from the villagers. I could almost hear the Haworth gossips wagging their tongues over tea: *The Misses Brontë's young boarder takin' up with Mr. Branwell! And him sent home in disgrace . . .*

For the short remainder of our journey, I was careful to maintain a distance between us. By the time we gained the garden, he appeared almost clearheaded. I grabbed him by the collar, pushing my face close to his, trying not to recoil from the piney smell of liquor.

"Remember—be pleasant!" I hissed.

He nodded. "I thank you, Miss Maria. In truth, I owe you greatly."

"Do not think on that now! Let us open the door ere we both freeze."

FAMILY MATTERS

Branwell's unexpected homecoming was hardly one of triumph. No laurels were placed on his brow; no welcoming words spoken. Emily shook her head, then went about her business, but Anne's horrified shock forced her into a chair. Mr. Brontë clenched his pipe, while Tabby muttered in disgust. Charlotte, who worked herself into a state, refused even to *look* at him.

He was bundled upstairs by Martha, followed by Mr. Brontë. The sisters exchanged a glance, uncharacteristically shutting the doors of their study behind them. Need I even make mention, Reader, that I pressed my ear to the wood, straining to overhear?

"He is as shameful a creature as ever lived!" cried. Charlotte. "The very sight of him disgusts me. What has he done *now* to merit expulsion?"

"Papa was in receipt of a letter." That was Emily—her affect flat as always. "From Mr. Robinson. He insisted that Brannie never again contact his family."

"What can be the reason?" Charlotte was loud and furious. "What further disgrace has he brought upon our heads?"

There was a silence, punctuated by the ticking of the large grandfather clock.

"I know." It was the quiet voice of Anne. "It is so bad, I cannot speak of it."

"Come, Anne! No need for such closeness. We are all three of us sisters."

"Yes. Well, I fear there was more than . . . friendship between Branwell and Mrs. Robinson. She is a wicked, wicked lady! And led poor brother on with professions of her love."

"Seductress! To take advantage of a vulnerable young man. Yet he himself should know better. He should have done his utmost to keep his passions in check!"

"But Charlotte, that has never been his character. He acts on the impulse of the moment. Surely you know this by now." Emily's tone was the same she employed for teaching..

Anne's faint voice sounded. *Couldn't she be bothered to speak up?*

"Mrs. Robinson is a bad woman. She must seek her own salvation. But what of Branwell? Is there anything to be done to save him from The Beast?"

Emily spoke immediately. "What if there is no Beast? No bright Heaven or sulphurous Hell—just the earth beneath us?"

"*Emily!*" both Charlotte and Anne rejoined.

"This talk of saving souls is pointless. What is to be done at present—*here*, on terra firma?"

Charlotte, who when it suited her could be practical, responded. "Let us see if he improves. Enough to secure a fourth position or at least do *something* useful. Let us not speak of *l'affaire* Robinson again. Perhaps his torment will lessen with the comforting march of time."

I heard Anne. "Does it ever?"

By the time the two doors swung open, I was seated at the pianoforte, busily practicing scales. None of the sisters addressed me as they dispersed in different directions.

I attempted with utmost discipline not to hit a wrong note, but the general mood was so glum, only Keeper acknowledged my efforts.

TAUGHT BY THREE GENIUSES

Over the next few days, the household anxiety rose like the east wind. Everyone was quiet, tiptoeing below stairs so as not to wake the inmate above. Mr. Brontë sat often with his son, and though I heard an occasional stir, but for the most part, all was silent.

The Misses Brontë enhanced their lessons, so I was engaged continually. Anne taught basic algebra, along with a bit of Italian; Emily read from Ovid's *Amores*, working with me on translations; and Charlotte plunged like a zealot into the teaching of French.

"*Est-ce que tu apprécies les oeuvres de Georges Sand?*"

"*Oui, Madame—je vous demande pardon, Mademoiselle.*" I must exercise caution! I had nearly erred by gracing her with the appellation: "Mme. Heger."

"*Qu'est-ce que tu aimes le plus?*"

"*Sa déscription de l'amour. C'est très franche et belle.* Miss Brontë, may I ask you a question?"

"Certainly. That is the foundation of learning."

"Why is it that the French portray Love with frankness, but such a thing is not to be tolerated here?"

"Yes." Charlotte's dark eyes blazed. "On the Continent, one might say there is more . . . sophistication. There, conventionality is *not* confused with morality."

"But—" I wanted to ask her if that is so, *why can't you declare yourself to ascertain if M. Heger reciprocates?* But then my sense intruded: after all, he *was* a professor of literature, bourgeois, and respectable. He did not have

the license of a Byron who could do whatever he pleased
. . .

March gave way to April, and gloriously with April came Spring. At last, winter cast off her cloak; a steady chill no longer weighted the air. I began to feel happier—lighter—as I loped Balthazar across the moors, marveling at the formerly hidden heath. I could not wait until September, when, Emily said, the purple heather would bloom.

Yet my high spring fever was broken by Haworth's most volatile inmate (if one could discount Charlotte, who normally kept herself regulated).

In the aftermath of his return, Branwell mostly hid in his room, occasionally venturing forth to the Black Bull and the druggist. Such habits were expensive, and he was endlessly in debt—endlessly begging his family for money. He dared not approach *me*, knowing his sisters would intercede. Still, I despised his weakness and pretended—like Charlotte—that he did not exist.

One afternoon, I was in the kitchen with Emily studying *The Aeneid*. At the same instant, the two of us were hit by the selfsame smell: an acrid burning wafting from the top storey!

We could hear Anne running downstairs before she appeared at the door.

"Fire," she told Emily. Evidently, she did not wish to disturb Mr. Brontë behind his closed study doors.

Emily seized a pitcher of water and vaulted athletically up the stairs. I panted as I sped after her. She ran into Branwell's room, unhesitatingly dousing him—as well as the bedclothes that flamed. Both she and Anne tried to rouse him, but he was proved insensible.

"D——n him!" Emily hissed. It was the matter of a moment for her to lift his prostrate form and fling it into a corner, along with smoking fabric. In another moment, the conflagration was quelled.

I stared up at Emily as if she were Aeneas. Never in my life had I witnessed such courage—such calm in the face of danger. Her outmoded sleeves and clinging skirt did not concern me now. I almost felt as if I should kneel and swear my eternal fealty!

Anne, trembling, had a different reaction. "Do not inform Charlotte," she begged.

"Nonsense. There are far too many secrets haunting this house as it is."

Charlotte was indeed told. That evening, she motioned me to remain when her sisters broke from dinner.

"Miss Maria," she began. I felt my muscles tense, for I could well surmise the subject of our tête-à-tête.

"As you are well aware, the composition of our household has altered. I fear that with its recent addition, The Misses Brontë's school must cease. One hopes this will cause little harm, as you *are* our solitary pupil."

"What of the harm done to *me*?" I cried, working myself into—I could hardly believe the phrase—a Brontë-like passion.

I stood at the dining room table.

"For the first time in my life, I am actually *learning*. I, who have been dismissed twice as many times as Branwell, find myself proficient in French—even Latin! I now know where the Urals stand. And what is seven times seven. I can play Liszt and draw a figure. Will you hurl me back into the Ignorance from which I have lately emerged?"

Charlotte looked tired and defeated. "In truth, I was not aware of your sentiments." She passed a hand over her brow. "However, Mr. Branwell's presence signifies the end of our school scheme. I have already written to your father."

"No!" I yelled. "Do you think I cannot handle Branwell? With one touch, I can immobilize him!"

Charlotte smiled at my bravado. "I do not doubt it, Maria. But we must not place you in jeopardy, as foretold by this afternoon's event. No, it is better that you leave Haworth—depart for London and its allure."

Reader, I had to struggle not to stare: never before had it struck me that a *Brontë*—with all their mental attainment—might envy me my old life. The two youngest seemed content in their seclusion, but Charlotte resisted burial—here at the end of the world.

I sought her wistful eye. "Could you not accompany me, Miss Brontë? As a sort of governess-in-chief."

She laughed. "My governessing days are past. I fear I was quite ill suited—not compliant enough to walk behind the master. In truth, I would much rather work as a housemaid."

"Oh, Miss Brontë!"

"Go. *You* were not made for suffering: not with wealth, station and beauty."

I felt my cheeks dampen—even startled her as I walked behind her chair, throwing my arms about her neck.

"I shall never forget you, Miss Brontë." I wished to follow my tears as they fell onto her head.

"Tu étais mon élève préféré."[6]

I understood. Mounting the stairs with a heavy step, I silently cursed Branwell. But then, as I reached my room, I found a smile crossing my lips. At that moment, I was formulating a plan—one that had all the hallmarks of being Brontësque.

---

[6] "You have been my favorite pupil."

A RAPID DECLINE

Following lessons with Anne the next day (I was now able to draw a bird without having it mistaken for a cat)—I departed the Parsonage on the pretense of taking some air.

Take it I did, after making my way down Main Street, navigating cobblestones with caution e, and entering the (very small) postal office.

"Ayup theear!" shouted the harried clerk, a young man who sorted through letters with the efficiency of a machine.

"Yes, how do you do." I reassumed my London airs. "I am here on an errand to seek a particular letter."

"Ain't everybody today?"

I ignored this. "I fear it was sent in error by Miss Charlotte Brontë of Haworth to Sir Shelby of 30 — — Harley Street, London."

"Ha!"

"In what way does that amuse you?" I adopted an icy stare.

"Well, Miss, tha' brother o' Charlotte cem roun' lookin' for dis sem letta, not 'un 'alf-hour agoa!"

His grin made his pale mustache look that much more ridiculous. "Ah reckon 'e can be fahn' a' t' Black Bull. Bur beware—'e wor real drunk when ah saw 'im!"

"Thank you. That will be all."

I dismissed him with a swing of my shawl and treaded downhill to the Bull. It looked quite a bit less gloomy (and sooty) in the bright light of spring.

"Hello." I approached a grimy boy lounging by its door. "What is your name?"

"Jimmy," he answered sullenly.

"Jimmy, could you please procure Mr. Brontë from within? Tell him that Miss Shelby wishes to speak to him." I leant down and whispered a second instruction.

"Alreight then." He shrugged and went in to perform his duty. I stood before that establishment for what seemed like a lengthy hour, observing men in varying states of dissipation.

At last, I beheld the sight I awaited: Jimmy emerging with his quarry, forcing him down the steps by maintaining an iron grip on his sleeve. Branwell seemed quite jolly and upon catching my eye, recited:

> In Xanadu did Kubla Khan
> A stately pleasure-dome decree:
> Where Alph, the sacred river, ran
> Through caverns measureless to man
> Down to a sunless sea.

"Ya know the poem, Missy Miss?"

"I do. It is 'Kubla Khan' by Coleridge. Samuel Taylor, to be exact."

"Ah, very good! My sisters have larned ya well! What else 'av ya larned?" He was broguing like the lone celebrant after Saint Patrick's Day.

"Why should that concern you? You do your best to destroy *your* learning."

"No, Missy Miss, no! Truly Oi swear it! Would yer like to hear another piece o' poesy?"

I gestured to my small emissary who handed up what I had bid him bring: a large mug of steaming coffee.

"Well, here it be." Branwell fortified himself with several gulps of the beverage, then started to declaim:

On Ouse's grassy banks—last Whitsuntide,
I sat, with fears and pleasures, in my soul
Commingled, as "it roamed without control,"
O'er present hours and through a future wide
Where love, me thought, should keep, my heart beside
Her, whose own prison home I looked upon:
But, as I looked, descended summer's sun,
And did not its descent my hopes deride?
The sky though blue was soon to change to grey—
I, on that day, next year must own no smile—
And as those waves, to Humber far away,
Were gliding—so, though that hour might beguile
My Hopes, they too, to woe's far deeper sea,
Rolled past the shores of Joy's now dim and distant isle.

He removed Jimmy from his person as I slipped the boy some coins for his service.

"Well, what do ya think?" Branwell asked, as he watched a joyful Jimmy clutch his bounty.

"Not much."

"Beg pardon?"

"It is maudlin and filled with self-pity. An homage to a 'love' that should not have been. The best line refers to your 'soul without control.' *That* is the truest thing there."

"Ah! So they've made ya into a critic! Ain't that gran'!" He sat down on the public house stairs.

"Pray do not bring to yourself more notice than you merit."

He made a sad drunken face, then shakily rose to his feet.

"Mr. Brontë, I have no more time to waste. I am informed by the postman that you possess a letter: one of great import to me. May I have it?"

"O'course!" he cried, withdrawing an envelope from his waistcoat. I snatched it from his unsteady hand.

"For what purpose did you remove this?" I asked.

"Because."

"Please—you are no longer a child, though you act the part."

"Brava! I stole the letter 'cause I don't wish to be the . . . the cause of your removal. You have improved considrab—much since you came. I will not contribute to a young girl's recidiv—ivism. *Comprenez-vous?*"

"Oui, moi aussi je comprends tout le monde à Haworth sait ton sort 'tragique'—au moins ta soeur—"[7]

"Which one?"

"Never mind."

This intelligence—along with the sobering brew— seemed to drive some of the liquor from his brain. "But *that* is not possible! They are incapable of attachment."

"Oh yes, that only applies to *you*! You and your precious suffering—"

"But I *do* suffer—"

"Oh, shut your head!" I must have looked as surprised as he did. "Cannot you see that you are acting the fool? That this Robinson woman professed her 'love' and desired nothing more than a . . . a . . . tryst with her adoring tutor—"

"Yet she sends me twenty pounds often."

"To keep you quiet, of course."

"She promised to leave her husband—"

"They all do! Are you not a reader of novels?"

---

[7] "Yes, I also understand that everyone in Haworth knows of your 'tragic' fate. At least your sister—"

As he began to sob, I softened.

"Believe me when I say I am not devoid of feeling. But I tell you that to continue down this path—this . . . this landslide—will lead only to tragedy. Perhaps the Ultimate one."

He wiped his eyes. "You have wisdom beyond your years, Miss."

"For Heaven's sake, call me Maria."

"Very well, uh . . . Maria. With your sagacity, you surely must have observed that I am a weak man. All I have attempted ends in disaster. I know I disappoint everyone: especially Father —and myself."

"Do you believe in predestination?"

"I—I don't know. It seems that God has written in his Book that it is *my* lot to fail."

"Pooh! I believe in no such thing. I think that every one of us possesses the will to change. We need only to exercise it."

"You are very young," he answered, walking with me toward Church Street, where the spire of Saint Michael beckoned. "Continue to learn all you can, since knowledge can stave off the dark."

"And the letter?" I asked, waving the envelope before him.

"I apologize. I do not know of what you speak."

He stuck out his hand and I shook it, sealing our thieves' bargain. There was something in having an accomplice that imbued Crime with a certain Thrill.

Yet when I conjured up Charlotte's face—lips pursed in a scowl, eyes flashing with disapprobation—I felt a second, more vibrant emotion: Fear.

APRIL 1844

A fortnight passed, and—astonishingly—there was *no reply* from Sir Shelby! I assured Charlotte it was probably due to his being abroad (if one could consider West Sussex a foreign land). At the Parsonage, affairs resumed as usual: I reviewed Dante with Anne—*in Italian*, finessed my writing with Charlotte, and even received a dose of German from Emily.

I could almost *feel* myself getting smarter, as if my skull pulled at its bony constraints in an effort to cram more learning inside. Despite the criminal act that insured my tenure here, I found myself quite content.

One afternoon when I was loping Balthazar, I spotted a lanky figure on the crest of a sloping hill. Emily. She was silhouetted against a farmhouse known locally as Top Withens. She stood stark and unmoving, at the side of two adjoined trees, as if taking the moors into her very veins. I did not wish to disturb her, but this was not to be: she had heard, from a distance, the pound of horse's hooves, each one the size of a dinner plate.

Feeling more than a little awkward, I trotted Balthazar over to where she stood.

"Do you not find yourself ridiculous?" were her first words.

I had grown used to her manner by now. "In what respect, Miss Emily?"

"Sitting sidesaddle on that brute! Would it not be more practical to ride astride as men do?"

"To be sure. But disapprobation counters the benefit."

"Name of God! You are in Haworth, not London. Do you think the simple folk here care a whit about your seat? Do it to please yourself."

She turned, staring at the horizon and the endless moors that stretched there in a distinct palette: red, gold, and brown. I could well understand why she wished to walk among them.

Knowing better than to bid farewell, I walked Balthazar off at a clop. On my way back to the Parsonage, I thought about her words. Despite the usual bluntness, she did have a point. I determined then and there to contrive a riding costume: one to allow me to sit the huge beast in comfort.

Granted, Emily was peculiar, but her mind was like a jewel. To what use was it put, I thought, beyond baking, scouring pots, and the teaching of one (semi-)ignorant girl? I sighed. It seemed such a shameful waste.

When I returned from my ride, spurred by Emily's views, I determined to stop "dressing like a princess." Even I could discern that my large skirts were cumbersome, and the finery I sported—rich silk shawls with tassels of gold—had never been admired. Certainly not by the Brontës. I recalled an expression that Charlotte had quoted from her great friend Mary Taylor: "It's like growing potatoes in a cellar." So I took my neglected crop and sowed its fields with something more nourishing.

Inside the secluded Parsonage, I served as another witness to Branwell's shocking decline. I understood from Martha that he regularly visited the druggist, and it was hardly for a cure: rather, lumps of opium. He spent his time not in a stupor ensconced at the Black Bull.

I rarely saw him now, for he staggered home in the wee hours to repair to his father's room (after the fire incident, he became Mr. Brontë's charge). The old man was forced to watch as his only son—once the family's great Hope —diminished into its shame. He did not give voice to his feelings, but bore all as stolidly as Job.

One evening, beset by guilt at Charlotte's deception, I heard Mr. Brontë's footsteps, pacing for hours in his room. Back and forth, to and fro—he must have worn holes in his wooden floorboards. At last, my stretched nerves begged me to act.

"Emily," I whispered at her door, but did not receive a response. I then knocked softly. When that yielded no result, I placed my hand on the knob and slowly swung open the door. I saw her sitting in bed fully clothed, scribbling on a small pad.

"Emily!"

"What?" she snapped at the interruption.

"It is three o'clock in the morning, and Mr. Branwell is not yet at home. I beg you to go out and fetch him from The Bull."

She shrugged. "He is a hopeless being."

"Yes, but you are *still* his sister. And the most able to execute this duty."

She sighed, then went out upon her errand, returning within the hour. She supported what seemed to me a lump of singing flesh. Confronted with utter ruin where there once had been such promise, I turned away my head, striving to quell my tears.

In years since, I have heard tell that Emily retrieved Branwell as she was the one most fond of him. Allow me to put this endearing—yet utterly false—rumor to rest. In truth, Emily cared little for the people of this earth, and much more for those she conjured in the imaginary land of Gondal.

As April came to its close, the weather stayed high and bright. This seemed antipathetic to Charlotte, who was assailed by migraine and weakness. I would not concede that her "illness" stemmed from the physical; rather, I believe it was wrought by *the post*, which never brought her a long-awaited reply.

As if in compensation, she continued her war on Branwell. She seemed to view him as unforgivable: his "religion and principle" lost. I heard her assault his character daily with all the zeal of a Dissenter.

The entire household suffered from its dissolute tenant. Anne had grown morose, spending hours alone in her room. When she did emerge, her sweetness was tempered with gloom. Emily's nights were consumed in serving as her brother's keeper. Even old Tabby shuffled about with markedly less of a twinkle.

It seemed clear (at least to me), that the Parsonage needed *something* to unloosen it from its torpor. As usual, it was I—the intransigent boarder—who played the role of instigator.

I was in the dining room, studying—the first part of *Il Divina Commedia*—when Tabby called from the kitchen.

"Someone fetch uz um yeast fra t' cellar!"

I glanced about. I was the only one downstairs. All of the sisters were either in their rooms or out.

"Ayup! Is anyone theear?"

"I shall do it, Tabby," I answered. I was quite determined not to be ruled by my fears.

I approached the small cellar door, attempting to summon a portion of Emily's fortitude. I descended the single flight, bracing myself by touching the adjacent wall. I heard a distant skittering, undoubtedly that of rodents. Although I was not a girl who shrieked at the sight of mice, I did not welcome their appearance either. Slowly, I made my way toward an ancient sack at the side of the fermenter, my outstretched arm trembling in the barely illuminated half gloom.

As a burlap string met my palm, *I heard it*! The sound of daemonic *cackling*, reverberating to the ceiling. I screamed, turning to dash up the steps. As I approached the narrow door, I could not resist—like Lot's wife, I looked back—and found myself greeted by the selfsame apparition as before—the ghastly black-and-white NUN!—features wrapped like a mummy; eyes gleaming from out their white bandage as she glided directly *toward me*!

I believe I was granted the power of flight as I ascended those last few stairs. I slammed the door shut, then collapsed onto Emily's chair and burst into a deluge of tears.

Tabby limped out of the kitchen with poor Martha at her side.

"Wha' int' nem o' t' lut 'as ap'n'?"

I could not speak through my sobbing.

"It mun av bin . . . *t' Nun*," Martha whispered.

"Aye—it's eur *ghost* who's 'auntin t' place!"

"No," I managed to get out. "She was as real as you or I—composed of solid flesh! Unless my mind has taken leave of me." I covered my face with my hands, my sobs coming even faster.

"There, there," said motherly Tabby. "These things ap'n int' North. Let uz gerr theur eur brew." She limped off, and I looked to Martha for clarity.

"She's gerrin theur teeur," she said brightly. I had been there long enough to intuit that tea would be brought.

At the dinner table that night, the sisters expressed skepticism toward my spectral friend. (Mr. Brontë, as was his custom, dined alone in his study, while Branwell hid above stairs.)

"So the phantom Nun reappears." Emily made a frightened face like a child.

"Perhaps . . . it is a sign." Anne broached meekly.

"Of what? A beer-seeking Sister of Mercy?" Emily was unconcerned if no one else was amused.

"A sign of what, Anne?" Charlotte attempted to humor her youngest sister.

"Perhaps . . . it is a warning. Sent to Brannie to punish him for his sins. It is a vision intended for *him*."

"All inebriates see visions. Yet plainly, our pupil is not of their number." Emily cheerfully downed a bite of mutton.

"Miss Maria. You pursue your work so vigorously. Perhaps you require a rest." Charlotte looked at me with concern.

"I am perfectly fine, Miss Brontë. I can still comprehend Dante and play badly on the pianoforte."

"Hmmm," said Charlotte, thinking. "I have lately received a letter from my old friend Mary Taylor. She has arrived—unexpectedly—from Germany. She extends an invitation for us to visit her at Hunsworth. Perhaps *you* could be one of our number."

"Thank you, Miss Brontë!" The prospect of seeing new scenery after four months of seclusion was not unwelcome to me.

All fears of the lurid vanished as I prepared a smallish bag, loaded with practical garb (though I did include a formal gown, for one *never knew*). I packed my Dante and Ovid, fancying myself quite the scholar.

I had heard much of Mary and wished to encounter her in the flesh. Was it possible that she—a former pupil in Brussels—could shed light my nagging query: what *exactly* had transpired there?

THE RED HOUSE

It was fifteen miles to Hunsworth Mills, itself situated in a town with the curious name of Cleckheaton. The Brontës had hired a gig, so our party of Charlotte, Emily, myself—*and Branwell*—squeezed into the light conveyance. Anne had remained at home to administer to her father.

Emerging from our cramped space, we found ourselves in a country dotted with rich forests and traced by the green-hued Spen. The house at which we alighted stood above the Taylor Mills and seemed—though not palatial—at least promising of comfort.

"Polly!" Charlotte greeted her friend, throwing herself into Mary's arms for a long, genuine hug. They had met at the Roe Head School when Charlotte was but fifteen, and had maintained a lifelong friendship ever since.

"Joe!" Charlotte shook Mary's brother's hand. Even Emily grunted a greeting, for she claimed she liked Mary, a person reputed to be as blunt as herself. Branwell merely bowed, embarrassed. He had sworn on his father's Bible to behave himself on this visit, and, after much hesitation, Mr. Brontë had relented: he felt that a change of air might do his prodigal son some good. To Emily fell the uncongenial task of minder-in-chief. I had heard that in earlier days, she had once guarded Ellen from a forward curate—hence her nickname "Major."

After freshening up, we were treated to a fine repast. Mary regaled us with tales of teaching boys (!) in Germany. She and Charlotte reminisced about old Miss Wooler, their headmistress at Roe Head. At last, Mary broached a topic that enflamed all of Charlotte's nerves.

"My friend, I must inform you that brother Waring and I have firmed our decision to emigrate. We have settled on Port Nicholson."

"But that's New Zealand!" Charlotte cried.

"Yes. I cannot bear further the treatment of our sex here. Especially those unmarried." She gave her friend a sharp glance.

"I beg you, Mary, do not desert me. You are my oldest, closest friend!"

"Hmmm—you *do* have two sisters, and what about poor Ellen? Have you not known her as long as me?"

Charlotte entwined her hands. "Yes. Yes of course."

Branwell, noting his sister's distress, said, "Let us move to a happier topic." Emily—a veritable human Keeper—sat ready to snatch his glass if he so much as looked at the wine. "Mary, apprise us of the local wonders."

"It would appear that brother Joe here is infatuated with one Miss — —."

"And what sort of person is she?"

"Only the most thoroughgoing flirt in Yorkshire!"

Everyone laughed as Joe colored. "I do hope to support her in the manner that she anticipates."

"In that case, better be knighted and steal a castle from Sir Shelby!" Mary smiled over at me.

"Pooh! You women talk nothing but nonsense— fanciful whimsy and tripe."

"And *that*—" said Mary, nodding in Joe's direction, "is why I am leaving England."

The party soon broke up, everyone in high spirits except the brooding Charlotte. She sat with her friend at one side of the drawing room, while I—a London proficient—positioned myself so as to be able to hear.

"Charlotte, you should join Waring and I. You are wasting away in Haworth."

"No, Mary, I have a duty to stay with Father."

"The selfish old man!"

"Mary!"

"I stand by my sentiment. Surely he knows he is burying his daughter at the end of the world."

"No, Mary."

"Have you envisioned what you'll be say in five years hence?"

"Yes. I am old now—nearly thirty—and as yet have done nothing, accomplished nothing."

"Then *why don't you*? You have more God-given talent than anyone I know."

Charlotte did not answer; she merely collapsed into sobs. Mary moved closer to comfort her.

This tête-à-tête left me perplexed. To what "talents" did Mary allude? Granted, Charlotte was a gifted teacher, but so were Emily and Anne.

As far as Charlotte leaving England, I found myself—not unnaturally—siding with my favorite. What did Mary expect her to do? Decamp to a faraway isle, leaving all friends—and cares—behind? I knew that Charlotte's character was such that she was strictly bound to her Duty: the more Branwell declined, the more firmly she clung to it. She would never abandon her father . . . or would she, if a certain professor appeared?

The next morning dawned dry and clear, so Joe Taylor proposed an outing: to Gomersal, two miles hence, to call upon his mother, who lived there as a solitary. Mary—whom I had already pegged a contrarian—proceeded to balk loudly.

"Pfft! If you want to see her, then go. For my taste, she is too full of moods since Father died. But, Joe, do take our guests—remove them from Hunsworth's dullness."

Charlotte demurred, wishing to spend more time with her friend, as of course did Emily, who despised all social activity.

Mr. Taylor therefore conveyed merely myself and Branwell to the Red House, where Mary had spent her youth. Its name was wholly appropriate, for it was composed of rich red brick. Cheery white casements led onto the lawn. Mrs. Taylor must have been sour indeed for the family to select Hunsworth over this charming alternative.

Mr. Taylor led us inside and introduced us to his mother. She immediately proceeded to rail at him for some imagined slight. I observed a painting behind her depicting an angry Vesuvius before I spotted Branwell creeping out the back. I made a move to follow. Then Inspiration struck me, and I, silent as my cellar persecutor, slipped unheeded out of the room.

I thought my heartbeat might give me away as I stole up the staircase. I found myself facing a gallery containing five rooms. I attempted to think like Emily: that is, *logically*. To my knowledge, Mary was the only female sibling (I would learn in later years that sister

Martha had died in Brussels). I therefore crept to the farthest room: the least desirable and hence the most likely to house a female occupant. I felt like Southey's old woman in the forest who intruded on three bachelor bears. . .

Triumph! This was clearly a girl's apartment: one that must have had sat vacant for an age. The lack of personal items, the too-clean rug, and naked bed all supported my conjecture. But *where* could I find the treasure—not of gold, but paper—which I thought might be buried in these deserted confines?

Reader, it is probable you are wondering: did I have a qualm of conscience as I played the intruder? A little. Though I lacked maternal influence, I was still a proper young lady and knew that my present course was irredeemably wrong. I wish I could plead derangement, but in truth on that day my mind had never been sharper . . .

I knelt, my modest skirt spreading around me, and examined the area beneath the bed's footboard; then pulled out each dresser drawer, finding nothing of interest: merely some yellowed handkerchiefs and an old pendant. I was now so embroiled in the lives of the Brontës that I was past correction and would have continued my course in the face of Scotland Yard!

I approached a tall wooden wardrobe and opened its double doors. The interior was sparsely populated, but it was not raiment that I sought. Impatiently, I laid some clothes on the bed, exposing a quantity of hooks affixed to a board that spanned a third of the armoire's width. I stood on tiptoe and ran my hand over the shelf guarding the hooks. *Nothing.*

Perhaps this quest was fantastic, born of the same haunted mind that could conjure a Spirit Nun. I felt worse than ridiculous. I paced the barren apartment, contemplating a swift withdrawal. If I departed now, no one would be the wiser.

Still, I lifted up a corner of the rug, freeing only a whirlwind of dust. I coughed, half expecting Mrs. Taylor to come thundering up the stairs. When she found me, would she be equipped with a kitchen blade in hand?

Steady, I told myself. On impulse, I went back to the room's largest occupant—the wardrobe—running my hand across every inch of its depths. After incurring a nasty splinter, I traced a fissure behind the small board itself. My fingers touched what I sought—a quantity of paper—wrapped tightly with a thin cord. I gave a vigorous tug, and the haphazard bundle was mine!

I let out a long breath, unbelieving of my good fortune. Tiptoeing over to the clothes-strewn bed, I sat, unloosed a cord, and began to peruse the envelopes. As I had suspected, the letters were all from Charlotte. Their addresses of origin varied as she herself changed location: Haworth, Rydings, Dewsbury Moor. But mostly they were from Brussels: the Pensionnat d'Demoiselles, 32 Rue d'Isabelle, addressed to Miss Taylor in Brussels, and then to her in Germany.

I determined to begin my reading with the recent past: 1843. Shakily, I took up a letter in a hand I well recognized. At first, Charlotte had been so happy to return to Belgium as a teacher—she described to Mary the fun of her English lessons and Monsieur's kindness as he lent her books. Yet the emotional climate had clearly changed by summer. Charlotte was left on her own for five weeks during "The Long Vacation," and, in her despair, actually entered a *Catholic church* and made a *full confession*. She dismissed it as "only a freak," but in my mind, I returned to her hatred of Romanists. Could this be the cause? *And what words had she spilled to the priest?* That poor man must have taken to the water of Lourdes!

The letters became more melancholic as the year progressed. Charlotte was no longer welcomed to the Heger's salon and did not speak to Monsieur, except on rare occasions. In October, she hinted to Mary that she knew the cause: "I fancy I begin to perceive the reason of this mighty distance & reserve: it sometimes makes me laugh, and at other times nearly cry. When I am sure of it I will tell <u>you</u> (<u>but</u> never <u>Ellen</u>)."

Proof of my suspicions! As I had surmised, Charlotte felt more comfortable unburdening her grief to Mary. From what I knew of Ellen, she sounded like a rather ordinary, dull woman. Of course, Charlotte would confide in a fellow intellect.

Her correspondence grew grimmer by the day. She was terribly lonely; alienated by the Hegers. Why did she not then depart for her home across the sea?

In a bundle of scrawled sheets, I found the answer to my inquiry. I sought to steady my hands as I sat on the bed, reading:

Pensionnat Heger
Brussels

12 December 1843

Dear Mary:

I am sorry to burden you again with my expatriate grieving—but of course I cannot tell Ellen, and even <u>Emily</u> may not serve as recipient of my confidence.

Knowing <u>your</u> acuity of mind, it is foolish for me to hide my feelings under subterfuge—indeed there is no one else to whom they may be imparted . . .

Madame H. hates me and works to drive me from her home because—for once!—her phlegmatic heart has discerned a woman's secret: <u>I am in love with her husband</u>.

I can conjecture this will not come as much of a shock—<u>to you</u>. It is the reason I returned to Brussels and continue to remain, despite Madame's—and her Army of Spies'—near hourly harassment. She has done everything in her power to remove me from Monsieur, short of actual <u>Murder</u>.

Yet I cannot help myself, Polly—you of all people know me. I am quick as Greek fire in temperament, which perfectly matches Monsieur's (I have indeed described him as a "bottled storm").

This is no schoolgirl crush, for I am long past the age of such things. In Monsieur, my Master— who rages like Zeus, but is no more to be feared than Flossy—I have found the one true Passion of my life: there has never been another nor <u>will there ever be!</u>

I know you are not easily shocked, Pag, whereas Ellen would have me banned from Church and most likely burnt at the stake! As I said, it cannot be helped: *"Un jour viendra où tout ce qui est dans ma vie aura changé, quand je ferai du bien aux autres, quand quelqu'un m'aimera, quand je donnerai tout mon coeur à l'homme qui me donnera le sien: en attendant je souffrirai en silence et garderai mon amour comme récompense pour celui qui me mettra en liberté.*"[8]

I am not mad enough—<u>yet</u>—to hope that my feelings are returned. Though I think that Monsieur cares for me—perhaps more than a little—there is nothing to be done while he is harnessed to Madame. I have described her to you as a woman of pedestrian mind, who creeps, ever so softly, in her foreign slippers, and I do believe, Pag, that my room has been "inspected"!

The bleakness of my situation—loving a married man—with <u>six children!</u>—strikes every minute at my soul and has led to nervous collapse and worse.

Oh Polly! I know that I should leave here—return to Haworth and Home at once—but the thought of abandoning Monsieur—never again to view his visage or speak to him in French—fills me with a despair I am simply unequal to face.

<u>Please, please</u> write as soon as you can—give me the strength to quit Madame's fortress ere I do something desperate and lose all semblance of sanity!

Love,

C B

I set down the letter beside me. Had such words ever been written—by *an Anglican clergyman's daughter*? It was

---

[8] "A day will come when everything in my life will be changed, when I shall do good to others, when some one will love me, when I shall give my whole heart to the man who gives me his; meanwhile, I will suffer in silence and keep my love as a reward for him who shall set me free." — George Sand

as if her pen had been dipped in fire, not so much moving across but *branding* every sheet! Why, oh why, had I started down this path? I was just as bad as Madame, though *my* footwear consisted of dependable English leather.

My breath came in spurts. This was not like reading George Sand, for that was fiction —*fiction*! This was all too real, involving someone I knew, someone I cared about deeply whose heart could never heal lest it be united with Monsieur's. For her, no other on earth would do.

I lost all sense of time as I sat there insensible. I might have been on the moon for all the awareness I had. Gradually, a pair of muddy boots came into focus before me. Looking up quickly, I saw they belonged to Branwell.

"Miss Maria, why is it that we always meet when pilfered letters are present?"

I shut my eyes, feeling my cheeks flame.

"No need to blush before *me*! Am I not a reprobate?"

"For once, let us not discuss *you*!" I cried. "I wish—how I wish—that I had never set eyes on these letters."

"Just fell on them by accident?"

"Do not seek to increase my shame. I already feel it sufficient."

"*I* know all about that." He pulled out Mary's old desk chair, placing it opposite the bed. Sitting, he asked, "What do you intend to do?"

"I will simply replace the letters and never think on them again."

"Harder to erase the memories of the heart." He sighed.

"What *is it* with you Brontës? Do you actively seek your own ruin? Compared to you, we Shelbys appear as angels." I brought up a sleeve to wipe my eyes.

Surprisingly, Branwell handed me his handkerchief. It was his most gallant gesture so far. I forlornly put it to my face.

"Allow me to lift your spirits, for I have *another* letter." He reached into his trouser pocket. There, in Charlotte's handwriting, was a wrinkled envelope—*addressed to Sir John Shelby*.

"My sister is not to be deterred," he said. "You should have seen her battle to study in Brussels. I'll give her that: she has the fortitude—and ambition—of any society woman."

I blinked. "I hardly envision her there."

"Yet *she* envisions herself—always has. She wishes to stand among her peers."

Before I could question him further, Branwell was off on his favorite subject—himself.

"In light of all that has passed, do you think me very bad, Miss? Utterly lost and beyond repair?"

For some reason, I could be frank with him—much more than with the bright young men of London. Perhaps *because* he was so unvarnished.

"I find your behavior of late worse than disgusting. You are mooning after a woman who is bribing you to keep silent while deluding yourself that *you* are the one she desires. You were a passing fling, no more—*une pratique amant*. Now that her husband knows, you have less worth to her than an insect which has flown."

He sighed. At least this time, he did not convulse into sobs.

"Further—"

He clutched his glasses in pain.

"—your collapse into drugs and drink accomplishes merely this: the complete waste of your talent."

"And what would that be?" he asked bitterly. "Being dismissed? Or failing as a painter of portraits?"

"You have the makings of a poet. I can say that now, since I have read the best—the Romantics, anyway. If you displayed one quarter of Charlotte's ambition, you could make a success."

"I think not." He lowered his head, brushing aside a red curl.

"And why is that?"

"Poetry is dying, Southey said. The greatest age is behind us."

"Write a novel then—is that *not* the popular form?"

"I wish I could." He sighed. "But the prospect of Death looms before me."

"*Nonsense!* You are not yet thirty, and your 'malady' is wholly of your own making."

"Still . . ." he twisted in his chair to look out Mary's bright window.

"Dwelling on dear Lydia? Exile her from your heart, for I guarantee she has already forgotten *you*."

He gave a low moan, then rose.

My eyes met his. "I trust you will not speak of this to anyone?"

He began to gesticulate wildly, which rather alarmed me. "Mason's honor!"

He and I worked silently to replenish Mary's wardrobe. I fastened the letters with their black cord, dropping them back to where I had found them.

"And what did you discover?" Branwell asked me of a sudden.

"Much more than I wanted to."

"That is the way with being a spy."

"Indeed, I know that now."

He nodded, and we each of us seized one door of the wardrobe, uniting then against further incursion. We stood for a moment with our hands on the handles, not more than six inches apart. My inner self issued a warning: I did not wish to prolong this intimate pose.

"Let us depart," I said. "Pray no one else discovers the letters."

As it happened, no one ever did. In future years, Mary, striving to protect her friend, burnt each and every one.

A Coach Journey with a Reprobate

Our visit to Hunsworth concluded with a gig ride back to Haworth. During our short stay, all had performed according to character: Emily was distant, spending most of her time at the Spen, though sometimes speaking to Mary; Charlotte was nervous and ill at the thought of her friend's departure; Branwell relapsed, staring vacant-eyed at the trees, no doubt in thrall to opium.

And myself? I was ashamed of my actions and swore off further entanglement in any of Charlotte's affairs. It was not an easy vow—for I *so* wanted to help her—but I would not abet adultery or dissolution of a home. To that depth I had not yet sunk.

The ensuing two months passed with little disturbance. Still no reply from Sir Shelby. *How could such a thing be?* Had he cruelly forgotten his daughter? Abandoned her to the North? Charlotte was so distressed she was determined to travel to London—*to speak with him in person.* Happily, this scheme was circumvented by *my* going to town, where—I promised faithfully—I would obtain a response directly.

I had now been at Haworth a half year, during which time my self-view had shifted from Prisoner to Happy Inmate. I was studying hard: learning philosophy from Emily and religious history from Anne. As I did not wish to quit the Parsonage, I told Charlotte that my ultimate goal was to teach (something I knew she much prized).

However, I doubted that even this would forestall my imminent leaving.

So I set out for London, having skipped Easter break in order to attend the party thrown for George upon his engagement. I was singularly unmoved by his fiancée, Miss Whatever-It-Was, but I *did* wish to see Isabelle and wear finery once again.

This time, a cart was hired to take me to Keighley, where another coach awaited. My designated male escort? None other than the degenerate Branwell!

At first I determined not to speak all the way to Leeds. However, he finally broke the silence.

"How do you do, Miss Maria?"

"Very well, I thank you." I could not hold my tongue. "I take it you are *not* intoxicated, since you seem to remember my name."

"Yes, Miss," he said stiffly, like one of Father's waiting men.

I smiled. "Let us not stand on ceremony. We have been through . . . too much together for that. How do you get on? I rarely see you these days."

"Yes, I have been ill—ill and cruelly used!" He glanced out the coach window from his seat opposite me. For once, he had bothered about his appearance, which extended to his having actually combed his hair.

"What is it now?" I tried mightily not to sound irritated.

"Mr. Robinson has passed—a fortnight ago."

"How brilliant for you! You may now marry a woman *seventeen years your senior.*"

He looked at me with incredulity.

"Yes, I do have ears. Why are you not at Thorp Green to claim your now free bride?"

"That wretched husband!"

"He is dead, you say? Perhaps he is happy now."

"Yes! But he put such a dreadful clause in his will—"

Lord help us, I thought.

"—if my sweet Lydia so much as *attempts* to contact me, she will be cut out entirely."

"And who relayed this intelligence?"

"William Allison, her coachman. He appeared at the Black Bull and told me that this stricture is driving her mad!" He put his head in his hands.

"Naturally."

For several moments, the only sounds to be heard were the squeak of polished leather and the ring of horses' hooves. "Did it ever occur to you that she is a *prevaricator*? That this story is mere invention to keep you at arm's length?"

"NO! It cannot be!" He clenched both his fists.

"It can, and I'll wager a goodly amount that it is. Put simply, dear Lydia is playing you for a fool."

"But she loves me!" he cried.

"She loves money," I answered. "Wait and see if the next husband does not have a pretty purse."

"You are very cynical for one of your young age."

"I am the daughter of a knight. I was raised among the privileged. Never underestimate the power of self-interest."

This seemed to take him aback. "But . . ."

We remained mostly in silence for the balance of twenty miles. I could not help but sneak a look at his brooding form. Really, he was not as unsightly as I had first imagined: though drawn and wasted now, his face still displayed a native intelligence and his light eyes a certain depth. I had even begun to accept his eyeglasses, and ginger—usually wild—hair.

After two more hours, Leeds Station came into view. The coachman handed me off, then carted my trunks toward the waiting train. I and my unlikely escort walked briskly to the platform.

"Well, good-bye then," I said, not wishing to hear one more syllable regarding poor dear Lydia.

"Farewell. You will return to us soon?"

"In six weeks. This is to be my midyear break."

"Well . . ." he thought a bit. "Don't fall prey to too much self-interest!" He bowed like a courtier and headed back to the coach.

I shook my head as I entered my car, presumably safe in the bowels of the iron horse. I had eleven hours' travel to London, and so picked up my text of Dante. My eyes settled on the famous phrase "Abandon all hope, ye who enter here." I wondered if for me the danger lay ahead or behind.

A Visit to Harley Street

At last, my journey was over. One carriage ride more, and I arrived at Harley Street. Our family reunion commenced. Emma must have been glad to see me, for she instantly stuck out her tongue; George gave me a hug, his eyes lively at the prospect of future bliss. Father came lumbering toward me as I took tea in the drawing room.

"Ah! Our Prodigal Scholar returns. I have had good reports, Maria—excellent, in fact. Miss Brontë wrote me in March that your progress surprises all. Odd that I have heard nothing from her since . . ."

"She is very busy, Father," I said, staring into my cup.

"No more buckets of water over headmistresses' heads?"

"Oh no, Sir! The Misses Brontë would never permit it. *Especially* Miss Emily."

"Capital. Appears to be just what you lacked— *discipline.* Have you learned to play Chopin yet?"

"No sir. But I can provide a sampling of Handel."

I strode over to our pianoforte—so much grander than the poor thing at Haworth!—sat down, and proceeded to play some notes that actually sounded like music. Father beamed, while Emma looked on in amazement. She even ceased torturing her puppy to listen. George smiled, but of course his thoughts were elsewhere: with the accomplished Miss —— (whose name I could still not recall).

Of course, it took inside of an hour for Isabelle to appear.

"Dear, dear Maria!" she squealed, hurling herself at me with the veritable force of Keeper.

"Isabelle," I responded. "I have not heard from you in ages. How are you?"

She led me over to a divan, practically seating herself on my lap. It was but a poor facsimile of the scene at Hunsworth: for Charlotte and Mary's friendship had long been forged in iron—not coal dust.

"I do apologize for being a desultory writer. The past few months have been frantic—first with your family at Briarwood, then endless concerts, engagements, and balls. I own I can barely stand!" She fanned herself with a hand.

"I hope you have been enjoying yourself," I said—and meant it. I waited for *her* inquiries.

"Oh yes! I am nearly beside myself, for Mother has ordered a gown from Paris. She refuses to tell me *anything*—the sweet tease. I expect it will be shocking!" She giggled, tossing her long dark curls.

"May your hopes come to fruition."

She must have noted my distant deportment, for she asked, "And how *is* our poor Maria? *Ecstatic* to be home, I am sure—away from those Northern brutes!" She patted my knee solicitously.

"Actually, events have proved otherwise."

"Indeed! Have you—" she lowered her voice, "—*an admirer*? Imagine finding such a one in a remote enclave!"

"You give me too much credit. I have no Haworth admirer. I merely meant that I now respect the Brontës and am learning much at their hands."

"But you *hate* to learn, my dear! Remember when you sewed your dress to a purse so you would not have to complete it? And hurled five cups of flour into a recipe, resulting in unleavened bread?"

"Of course." I smiled. "But the subjects I study at present do not require needle and thread, nor a measuring cup."

Isabelle attempted to absorb my report. "How ... extraordinary. You have not forgotten how to dance, I trust, for George's party is tomorrow."

"Indeed, I have not."

"Wear your prettiest frock, for there will be young men by the dozens! Alfred and Colin, to be sure, and all of George's Cambridge friends."

I nodded.

"You seem quite restrained, my dear. Almost ... *older*. Now, shake off that solemn face and help me eat these chocolates."

I did as I was instructed. I determined not to draw undue notice—quite an alteration from my old exhibiting days. When I work on the morrow, I saw that the weather gods had clearly favored George. In London, one never knew: the deities might just as well conjure rain, in which case the party would remove indoors.

This calamity averted, I joined a long receiving line in Father's verdant back garden. Indeed, the space fairly shone: with impromptu white tents shielding tables and chairs; and large stripped umbrellas to shelter pale complexions. All of the women looked cool in their light, pastel frocks. *I* wore nothing grand (for London): just a blue muslin dotted down the front with buttons.

"There she is! So the savages haven't consumed you?"

I smiled as Alfred and Colin approached, drinks casually in hand. They both looked exactly as the same as they had at Christmas.

"What is the word from the uncouth North?" asked Alfred. As usual, he was the best-dressed gentleman there.

"Do ya tawk lak dis no', lass?" Colin flashed a brilliant smile, aware as always that he was the handsomer of the pair.

"You would be amazed at the couth that exists there." I turned toward Colin. "You are able to comprehend me?"

They both laughed heartily. Colin took a small step forward.

"And there is not to be a second announcement today?" He hesitated. "Of your own future betrothal?"

"I am not to be married, Colin."

"Well, that *is* a relief!" Alfred jostled for position. "No Yorkshire admirer then? No mill worker or Master?"

"The only mill I know belongs to the Taylor family. And Mr. Taylor is quite transfixed: by a reputed local flirt."

They both lifted their glasses. We continued our light banter, but what did it really mean? All this talk of suitors and marriage: did anyone here ever think on *anything else*? Even I, as a denizen of England, knew that matrimony would be my expected fate. Still, I possessed an advantage over women like the Brontës: I was rich and, therefore, could afford to wait.

Isabelle flounced over with a gentleman I did not know.

"Miss Shelby, please allow me to present Lord Nigel Kirby. His father is Duke of M——, and so incredibly rich!"

Lord Kirby appeared unabashed at this gauche introduction. I therefore dismissed him in my mind as a grander version of Alfred.

The day unfolded pleasantly enough: the weather held; the cold luncheon was superb; and George looked the picture of happiness, his arm about Miss — — (I fear I never did learn her surname).

She was the sister of one of his Cambridge friends and of a lower station: that is, her father possessed a Title without the requisite Money. This was considered an excellent match—for her. One could not forget, for everyone kept repeating it.

As the afternoon lengthened, my desire for anonymity was thwarted by a group of women gathering round the bride-to-be (her first name, I knew, was Athena). This party cooed in unison as various gifts were unwrapped, most intended for a future household. Athena then opened a box and unfolded a red silk handkerchief. Embroidered on the material was this ornate script: *"Quid Amor iussit, non est contemnere tutum; regnat et in dominos ius habet ille deos."*

"How . . . lovely," she said. The whole assemblage looked blank. "Yet I wonder as to the meaning?"

I was now so conditioned to answer that I did so without hesitation. "'It is not safe to despise what Love commands. He reigns supreme and rules the mighty gods.' Ovid."

The whole company stared as if I had just arrived from Cape Town.

"And what language *is* that?" queried a stern-faced woman.

"Latin."

I heard whispers all around me—some matrons even stepped back in case I carried an unknown plague.

"She knows Latin," a voice whispered.

"Scandalous."

"And *her father* a Shelby!"

The group parted around me like a latter-day Red Sea, carrying Athena with it. I stood by myself, inwardly cursing my public display. I would have to be circumspect—in *this* company at least—and not reveal my other accomplishments. If word went about that I knew Dante and division, I might—as Charlotte had written—be banned from the very Church. Or perhaps thrown into Newgate as an "unnatural" woman.

As it pertained to Knowledge, *the Brontës* were the fortunate ones, through a quirk of geography: isolated in Haworth, they could maintain their mental liberty, and no one would be the wiser. As school mistresses, it was hardly suspect for them to be in possession of a mind.

As to myself, in London, I must lead a dual existence, the learning of the past half year hidden like Charlotte's letters. I had never been obliged to hide my real self (except for the mischief and pranks) but that self was much altered now. I must exercise due caution. I tried to summon a smile as George and Father approached, determined to become, if I wasn't already, a resolute dissembler.

A CHANGED MAN

I remained at home for the full six weeks and, by the last one, could hardly wait to depart. I had been subjected to Isabelle and Lord Kirby's "connection" (though *she* appeared far more invested than he); Emma's tantrums and spoiling; and Athena Surname-Escapes-Me's striving to endear herself as "my sister."

I did appreciate her effort, though not the actual result. She herself was pleasant enough: a relatively poor girl who had ensnared the golden goose. But her attempts at ingratiation nearly caused me physical pain. Had she not tried so hard, I might have felt some affection: but her constant hovering, arm pats, and whispers made Isabelle look like a Gnostic.

I did not require another sister—and not just because of Emma. *The Brontës* were sisters enough, and these at least I respected. I found myself longing for their world and not so much my own, even with the incessant balls, banquets, and near-constant amusement.

At the finish of July, the day came at last to return to London Bridge station. I had said my farewells to George, promising I would return in good time for his wedding; given Emma a kiss; and obtained from Father an envelope—addressed to Miss C. Brontë.

For the second time, I endured the train ride to Leeds. Again, a waiting coach dropped me off at Keighley. I did not know whom to expect: would it be Anne and Emily, perhaps augmented by Charlotte? Or Martha, still young enough to trek across the moors?

I smiled as I saw Branwell, but how *changed* in appearance! He looked like he had undergone a struggle, and it was not yet apparent that he had been the victor. His skin was pale and mottled, his eyes behind glasses dim, and it seemed to me that he had lost at least two stone.

"Branwell! Are you ill?" I forwent a usual greeting.

"I have been." He managed a weak grin. "But I am nearly better. There was a week or two, Miss Maria, when I earnestly wished for Death and would have been glad to receive his hand."

"Do not say such a thing!" I cried. "What happened?"

"I . . . I decided to quit my habits to make something of my life. As . . . as you so astutely stated. Giving up drink was not easy, but the withdrawal from opiates? It is a fate I would not wish on the very Devil."

I stood completely still as I absorbed this report. I could not fancy—even in dreams!—that my words had spurred him to halt his intemperate ways. Wordless, I walked to his side as he took up my trunks, and we treaded the path to Haworth. At last, I recovered enough to speak.

"I am so—so happy to hear this news! It is the best I have received over these long six weeks."

"London not as dazzling as formerly?"

"No, rather tedious. But let us turn to you! Now that you are cured, what have you been doing? Devoting yourself to poetry?"

"No time for that," he said ruefully. The dry yellow heath of the moors rose around us on all sides. It was like walking on the sun.

"I am currently in Bradford, studying with my former patron Mr. Leyland. I am working with all my might to become a painter of portraits."

Shyly, he withdrew a miniature canvas from beneath his low-slung vest. I stared at the subject's visage, expecting to find a Brontë; instead—there could be no mistake—the girl smiling in paint was none other than myself!

I turned away, feeling my cheeks burn.

"No need for that, Miss—uh, Maria. I searched for a suitable subject and thought at once of you. My family has posed *ad nauseam*, and they could not be persuaded again!"

I laughed. I had seen that early work hung about the Parsonage and could not state in all honesty that the figures were like. *This* new piece, however, struck me as a great improvement.

Branwell attempted to hand it to me.

"No, I couldn't." All of my antennae rose at the thought of accepting a gift— from a male who was not family. ("It cannot be sanctioned, my dear," echoed the voice of old Miss M——. "Indeed, it cannot be *done*.")

"It is all right," he said, pressing the canvas into my arms. "As you said in the coach, we have been through so much together. In sheer power of crime, do we not rival the Jacobins? I wish to reward the being who inspired my own redemption. Please, turn it over."

He dropped back onto the path. I carefully reversed the portrait, reading the neatly penned script.

To Miss Maria Shelby:

She walks in beauty, like the night
 Of cloudless climes and starry skies;
And all that's best of dark and bright
 Meet in her aspect and her eyes . . . .

"Byron," I said weakly, but did not feel so much the eager pupil now. A riot of feeling shot through me, and I did not know how to respond. Did Branwell seek to join my small circle of "admirers"? Or was quoting Byron mundane to him, as sure as washing his face?

I stopped, turning to face him. "Thank you," I got out. "Thank you very much." And then: "It is beautiful. I shall treasure this gift always."

He smiled to the tip of his beard.

At that moment, I recalled urgent business that must be done ere we arrived at the Parsonage.

"Branwell," I said abruptly, "you are an accomplished artist. Do you think you can feign the script of another?"

"I did all the time at Luddenden Foot."

"Good." I withdrew Father's envelope. "Are you able to emulate this hand? I believe you can surmise the contents."

"Of course!" Once more, we were Brother and Sister in crime. I produced a brand new sheet, along with pen and ink. He soon set to work, using my back as an improvised desk. With a flourish, he completed the fraud, and I slipped the counterfeit letter into its receptacle.

We walked on in near silence until we came to the Parsonage. How much cheerier those grey stones looked in the slanting beams of Summer!

"Here I shall leave you. I must return to Bradford." Branwell set my two trunks down on the top step. "Emily can help you with that."

"You are going to *walk*?"

"Why not? It is but a mere ten miles!" He waved and set off, whistling.

I shook my head and knocked. Martha stepped out to greet me and I could see the warmth in her eyes. After my long sojourn in London, I was finally Home.

STILL NO REPLY

I found the three sisters in the dining room, just completing their meal. They all greeted me with a smile: even "Major" Emily. I could tell at a glance that Charlotte was ill, with the cause easily surmised: still no reply from Monsieur.

I decided not to delay and presented "Sir Shelby's" letter. Charlotte ripped open the envelope and read aloud these words:

"22 July 1844
"Sir Richard Shelby
"30 — — Harley Street
"London
"Dear Miss Brontë:

"I regret I have been remiss in addressing your various correspondences. I sincerely beg your apology, as business had called me abroad, and I do not employ a secretary. Please allow this letter—hand-delivered by my <u>dearest daughter</u> Maria—to serve as my single reply.

"Miss Brontë—I have not failed to detect a discernible change in my daughter, and it is all to the better! She now plays upon the pianoforte, draws tolerably well, and contains somewhat more in her head than vacancy. To your tutelage do I ascribe this.

"Therefore, the illness of Mr. Brontë does not concern me in the least. Provided that he is not actually <u>contagious</u>, I am confident that yourself and the other Misses Brontë are quite capable of handling the matter. Further, I hear glowing reports from Maria that your brother is quite the charmer, brilliant as a young Keats, and spilling over with talent."

(*That Branwell!*)

"In sum, I strongly desire Maria to continue at your school until she knows as much as her horse. Though her station in life is high, it *is* conceivable she might one day employ her mind on something other than ordering dinner."

(*Branwell!*)

"I proffer to your whole household my wishes for your good health. <u>Please G–d that Mr. Branwell recovers!</u> I shall pray for him day and night. Kindly extend my warmest greetings to that reputed pillar of warmth, the Rev. Mr. Patrick Brontë.

"With Utmost Regard,
"Sir Richard Shelby, Knight
"Upholder Of Her Majesty's Glorious Empire"

Did he *have to* include that last line? And Father's given name was "John," not Richard! Still, Charlotte seemed convinced: by both the hand and its effusions. She shook her head a few times, then slipped the letter into a book. I confess I espied some other—hastily scrawled—sheets occupying that space.

Reader, I do not presume to own the power of prognostication, but I can well conjecture your thoughts. They must be along the lines of *"No, this cannot be! She is not* going to read another of Miss Brontë's letters after vowing to forego the practice."

If I had been strictly a person of honor—like Anne—I would have passed by that volume, to note its presence no more. But *because* I am a person of honor, I must—in accord with Charlotte's own strictures—convey to you in this book the Truth as I understand it. To do less would be to belittle you.

I waited for the whole house to retire (the sisters took to their beds far later than Mr. Brontë), pretended to read in the meanwhile, then crept up to that book and opened it. Yes, it was dishonorable, but I was in thrall to my interest as surely as Branwell had been to opium.

As I perused the letter, my French was now so improved that I barely consulted my Dictionary.

24 July 1844
Haworth

Monsieur:

I am well aware that is not my turn to write to you, but since my old friend Mrs. Wheelwright is going to Brussels and is willing to take charge of a letter -— it seems to me that I should not neglect such a favorable opportunity for writing to you . . . .

I scanned down the page, skipping long passages about her plans for the school and her own writing:

> . . . . that is why I refrain from uttering a single complaint about your long silence—I would rather remain six months without hearing from you then add an atom to your burden . . . .
>
> . . . Ah Monsieur! I once wrote you a letter which was hardly rational, because sadness was wringing my heart, but I shall do so no more—I

will try to stop being egotistical and, though I look on your letters as one of the greatest joys I know, I shall wait patiently to receive them until it pleases and suits you to send them. But all the same I can still write you a little letter from time to time—you have given me permission to do so.

Goodbye Monsieur—
Your grateful pupil,
C. Brontë

There was a postscript.

July 24th.
I have not asked you to write to me soon because I don't want to seem inopportunate but you are too good to forget that I wish it all the same—yes—I wish for it very much—that is enough—after all, do as you please, Monsieur—if in fact I received a letter and thought that you had written out of pity for me—that would hurt me very much . . . .
. . . once more, good-bye, Monsieur—it hurts to say good-bye even in a letter—Oh, it is certain that I <u>shall see you again one day</u>—it really has to be—for <u>as soon as I have earned enough money to go to Brussels I shall go</u>— <u>and I shall see you again if it is only for a moment.</u>

My God! She might as well have declared herself as frankly as she had to Mary. I replaced the sheets by "Sir Shelby's," feeling somewhat lightheaded. I padded into the kitchen, pouring water from a pitcher into a cup. All the while, I lost myself in Charlotte's plight: *Why oh why did not Monsieur write back?* Would it have *killed* him to send a few lines even on some mundane matter? But no. I understood his position. Letters such as Charlotte's were not "catch-ups" from an ex-pupil. It would be as if I wrote flaming prose to Branwell, quoting Byronic stanzas and vowing that I would die if we were apart!

Why was *I* conflating myself with Charlotte? *I* was not writing such letters. *I* was not acting to earn censure (in a purely romantic sense—certainly I was wrong to peruse the private letters of another, and, while on the topic, to commission the forging of same!). But *should I* have been doing something? Should I be taking a cue from Charlotte? I walked into the darkened hallway lit only by my nighttime candle. I headed toward the Parsonage entrance, overcome by the absurdity of my own Imagination.

There was no hope for me and Branwell: it was just as unlikely a match as Charlotte and her married Monsieur. I was who I was and would never—not in a century!—be permitted to marry so far below my station. *My duty* was to emulate Isabelle: ensnare some duke or earl and entwine the two family fortunes. My only course was delay; still, the inevitable would come—in fact, would be demanded.

I took up my small portrait, smiling as I reread Byron's lines: "'She walks in beauty, like the night ....'" Such beautiful words. And it *was* a beautiful night. If I possessed the authorial genius of expression, I would write:

> ... that sky expanded before me,—a blue sea absolved from taint of cloud; the moon ascending it in solemn march; her orb seeming to look up as she left the hill tops, from behind which she had come, far and farther below her, and aspired to the zenith, midnight-dark in its fathomless depth and measureless distance; and for those trembling stars that followed her course; they made my heart

tremble, my veins glow when I viewed them. Little things recall us to earth; the clock struck in the hall; that sufficed; I turned from moon and stars . . . .[9]

The clock on the landing struck as I held my candle before me, ascending the stairs to my room.

---

[9] Charlotte Brontë – *Jane Eyre*

VOLUME II

THE LAST WORD

Time passed, as it always does, until I had spent *a full year* at The Misses Brontë's Establishment. Another harsh winter descended, and I seldom ventured abroad. This acted not as an impediment but rather as a stimulus to my studies.

My knowledge of French was near fluent, and—though not a Newton—I had a basic concept of how the world worked (and even that it spun on its axis!). Anne and I had lively debates on Dante (I preferred Milton's Hell, but she was partial to the Italian's). Emily lectured on Kant and Hegel, and though I could not grasp the *whole* of the meaning, I at least made progress in German.

With Charlotte I worked on my writing, which became more than abysmal. She was the *first*—and only—Master of Literature I ever had. *Did one require another after Charlotte Brontë?*

Branwell continued at Bradford, and I saw him only infrequently. When he walked the ten miles home, he seemed eager, though somewhat discouraged. He was learning much from Leyland, but paid commissions were few.

"Such is life in the arts," he said. Truer words have never been spoken.

I continued to fret daily over Charlotte's mental state. Mrs. Wheelwright was back from Brussels but with no reply from Monsieur. I knew that Charlotte wrote again in November: again, no reply. I attempted as best I could to distract her—even asking questions to which I knew the response—but *no one* could relieve her pain.

Her eyes emitted near sparks as she haunted the household, as divisive a figure as Branwell in his fire-starter days. It seemed to me that Anne and Emily—whom Ellen had called "like twins"—grew ever more attached, and, if possible, more reclusive.

Charlotte's fury rose to its height shortly after the new year with her last letter to Monsieur, which must have burnt his hands as he opened it. This one I did not steal—it was given willingly—*much later, as you will see*—and here is the very text, copied from the original:

Haworth—Bradford—Yorkshire
8 January 1845

Mr. Taylor returned. I asked him if he had a letter for me—"No, nothing." "Patience"—I say—"His sister will be coming soon"—Miss Taylor returned. "I have nothing for you from M. Heger" she says "neither letter nor message."

When I had taken in the full meaning of these words—I said to myself what I would say to someone else in such a case "You will have to resign yourself to the fact, and above all, not distress yourself about a misfortune that you have not deserved." I did my utmost not to cry not to complain—

But when one does not complain, and when one wants to master oneself with a tyrant's grip—one's faculties rise in revolt—and one pays for outward calm by an almost unbearable inner struggle.

Day and night I find neither rest nor peace—if I sleep I have tormenting dreams in which I see you always severe, always saturnine and angry with me—

Forgive me then, Monsieur, if I take the step of writing to you again—How can I bear my life unless I make an effort to alleviate its sufferings?

I know that you will lose patience with me when you read this letter—You will say that I am overexcited—that I have black thoughts etc. So be it, Monsieur—I do not seek to justify myself, I submit to all kinds of reproaches—all I know—is that I cannot—that I will not resign myself to the total loss of my master's friendship ... If my master withdraws his friendship from me entirely I shall be absolutely without hope—if he gives me a little friendship—a very little—I shall be content—happy, I would have a motive for living—for working.

I skipped over a paragraph that appeared to deal with the poor until I arrived at the letter's end:

I don't want to reread this letter—I am sending it as I have written it—Nevertheless, I am, as it were, dimly aware that there are some cold and rational people who would say on reading it— "she is raving"—My sole revenge is to wish these people—a single day of the torments that I have suffered—then we should see whether they wouldn't be raving too.

One suffers in silence so long as one has the strength and when that strength fails one speaks without measuring one's words too much. I wish Monsieur happiness and prosperity

After this came a scrawled coda in English.

I must say one word to you in English . . .
(*about having heard French spoken in Bradford*)
. . . every word was most precious to me because it reminded me of you—I love French for your sake with all my heart and soul.
Farewell my dear Master—may God protect you with special care and crown you with peculiar blessings
C. B.

Has any woman alive loved with the heat of Charlotte Brontë? And what's more, is capable of expressing it in words that singe the skin? I know of no other—save Emily—but *her* lovers are phantoms from an imagined world.

Charlotte however was real, and the black pall of her moods hung over the Parsonage. I saw a decided change in her after she sent that last letter: she knew her campaign was over and had been sent to smoking defeat. She became ill more frequently, with headache, toothache, and cough. And what was *I* to do but stand helplessly by?

A full half year unfolded as Charlotte continued to sink. She worked hard at self-regulation, but all—even Mr. Brontë—must have felt her distress. Even a three-week visit to Rydings (and Ellen) did little to raise her spirits.

One evening near the end of July, I was walking past Anne's room and heard voices from within. The other belonged to Emily.

"I am weary of writing on Gondal." That was Anne.

"How so? They are in *excellent* playing condition."

A deep sigh from Anne.

"Very well—let us read our Diary Papers."

"We are not permitted to open them until three years hence! *That* is the agreement."

"Just read a little for my amusement, and I shall do the same."

"Very well." I heard the unfolding and crinkle of paper, followed by Anne's voice.

"This regards Thorp Green: 'During my stay I have had some very unpleasant and undreamt of experience of human nature.' Also: 'Charlotte is thinking about getting another situation—she wishes to go to Paris—Will she go?'

'I wonder how we shall all be and where and how situated on the thirtieth of July 1848 when if we are all alive Emily will be just thirty I shall be in my twenty-ninth year ... what changes shall we have seen and known and shall we be much changed ourselves? ... I for my part cannot well be flatter or older in mind that I am now ....'"

"How excessively cheerful."

"It is now *your* turn to read."

Emily cleared her throat. "Yes. You will observe that mine is like sunshine compared to your shade: 'I am quite contented for myself—not as idle as formerly, altogether as hearty and having learnt to make the most of the present and hope for the future with less fidgetiness that I cannot do all I wish—seldom or ever troubled with nothing to do and merely desiring that everybody could be as comfortable as myself and as undesponding and then we should have a very tolerable world of it—'"

They both laughed. I tiptoed past on the way to my room. It was telling that Anne felt family grief, while Emily glided along, enrapt in her own self. I was sorry they had not discoursed more on Charlotte, but this topic, perhaps, had already run its course.

PASSION

As July passed into August, I rode Balthazar across the greening moors. I told myself that I required fresh air and exercise, which was ostensibly true; however, I must confess that I cantered the low-lying hills in the hopes of seeing Branwell.

We had not met for several weeks as he continued his study in Bradford. Seven years prior, he had made a selfsame—but failed—attempt. I prayed every morning that *this time* would prove a success, for I did not wish to have him consumed by the dragons of drug and drink. Reader, if I possessed a secondary motive, I was not willing to admit it—even to myself.

One night, about twilight (for the sun did not set until nine), I loosened the reins for Balthazar so that he could carry us home. As he wheeled on a gentle lookout, I espied a familiar figure trudging the path to Haworth. There was no mistaking that steady gate or the gentleman's flame-red hair.

Turning my unwilling mount, I loped him to the man's side.

"Good evening, sir!" I greeted him, bowing my uncovered head. I had been riding an hour, and my hair must have been wild. "Do you have leave to be walking this country near dark?"

He laughed. "As much as *you* have to be riding it."

I stepped off my mount, leaping the considerable distance to the ground. I allowed the reins to dangle, for Balthazar had long proved worthy of my trust.

Branwell and I faced each other awkwardly. "How goes the future member of the Royal Academy of Arts?"

"As destined not to arrive as last time." I had heard tell of this misadventure: as a young man—and the Great Hope of the Brontës—Branwell had started off for London with his best work in tow. Alas, he never attained his object: his journey had reputedly ended at the bottom of a glass of gin.

"Well . . . perseverance and all that." I shrugged, trying to sound cheerful.

"It is of no use: the truth is, I am a middling painter of portraits." He looked down at his dusty boots.

"*Write* then." I sounded desperate, and not just for him.

"A novel takes time and energy. It is *not* an easy feat. And meantime, I must make some kind of living. I am nearing thirty and still a burden upon the parish."

He put his hands to his eyes. "I had so much promise as a youth! How I have failed . . . everyone, everyone." I saw his shoulders shake as he began to sob. To the west, the bottom edge of the sun touched upon hills bursting with wildflowers.

"Now, now," I said, wondering what Charlotte would do. I was so unused to a man expressing emotion that I stood as if stricken by pestilence. Yet the figure before me was greatly in need of succor.

I approached as I would a smoldering blaze, placing a tentative hand on his shoulder. With one move, I was somehow in his arms, pressed against him as if we were one.

"No, you mustn't!" I cried. His response was to draw me back slightly, then press his lips against mine. I had never been kissed before and I found myself eagerly opening my lips, placing my hands around his head, and caressing his thick, rough hair.

He bent me back, and his fine painter's hand wandered down my riding shirt, freeing it from my trousers and touching the flesh beneath with a fervor that made me cry out.

"Stop! Enough!" I disentangled our two bodies, amending my shirt back to its proper place, my breath beyond my control.

"Why?" he asked, puzzled. "Do you not love me?"

"Of course I do!" I watched him readjust his glasses and put a hand to his breast to regulate his own breathing.

My injured female vanity obscured all before me. "Do you think me a Mrs. Robinson, content with the role of courtesan?" I could hardly believe the frankness of my own speech.

"No, no—not at all! I love you—*you alone are my soul mate*—and I want to marry you. Maria, please, be my wife and life's partner!"

I could feel the sudden tears fall. "Can you not see that *we* are as hindered as shameful Lydia and yourself? That there is an obstacle between us that cannot be surmounted?"

He looked confused. "Are you already affianced?"

"Of course not! Did it not occur to you that *I* am very rich, and *you* have no income or fortune? Father will never agree—in his eyes, such a union is *a disgrace*. To the Shelby name." I had now begun to sob freely.

He took my hand in both of his. "And is it really so dire?"

I nodded. "We must cease to meet. Forget the other's existence."

"I could as soon forget my own!"

I seized my hand from his grasp, and, using the leverage of a boulder, took a mighty leap onto my horse.

"I beg you—*do not enter the Parsonage. Never speak to me again!*"

I wheeled my giant steed to see Branwell kneeling on the path, head sunk to his breast. I galloped back to the Black Bull as if I sat a thoroughbred, but my aim was not to race: rather, to escape.

DISCOVERY

Branwell heeded my words, and I—the resolute dissembler—went about my usual regimen. I continued to learn, hiding my great hurt; Charlotte continued to teach, so heavyhearted that I feared she might break down.

Who in the great wide world could have predicted that *Emily*—of all people!—saved us and made us embrace a calling far beyond ourselves?

It all began with a Discovery. Charlotte and I were in the sister's study—my assignment was to write in French on the new *Three Musketeers*.

While I worked, I observed Charlotte from the corner of my eye: She rose, stretched, then picked up a small notebook sitting on Emily's chair. She opened it and commenced reading. After several minutes, I heard her exclaim, "Oh my God!"

For Charlotte—the devout clergyman's daughter—to blaspheme, the earth must have shifted its axis. I looked up with incredulity.

"Maria—" for she called me that now, "I wish you to listen to this!" She recited from the notebook, her voice soaring with each subsequent stanza:

> Cold in the earth—and the deep snow piled above thee,
> Far, far, removed, cold in the dreary grave!

Have I forgot, my only Love, to love thee,
Severed at last by Time's all-severing wave?

Now, when alone, do my thoughts no longer
hover
Over the mountains, on that northern shore,
Resting their wings where heath and fern-leaves
cover
Thy noble heart forever, ever more?

Cold in the earth—and fifteen wild Decembers,
From those brown hills, have melted into spring:
Faithful, indeed, is the spirit that remembers
After such years of change and suffering!

Sweet Love of youth, forgive, if I forget thee,
While the world's tide is bearing me along;
Other desires and other hopes beset me,
Hopes which obscure, but cannot do thee wrong!

No later light has lightened up my heaven,
No second morn has ever shone for me;
All my life's bliss from thy dear life was given,
All my life's bliss is in the grave with thee.

But, when the days of golden dreams had
perished,
And even Despair was powerless to destroy,
Then did I learn how existence could be cherished,
Strengthened, and fed without the aid of joy.

Then did I check the tears of useless passion—
Weaned my young soul from yearning after thine;
Sternly denied its burning wish to hasten
Down to that tomb already more than mine.

And, even yet, I dare not let it languish,
Dare not indulge in memory's rapturous pain;
Once drinking deep of that divinest anguish,
How could I seek the empty world again?

"Oh my God!" I cried, echoing Charlotte. "'Fifteen wild Decembers . . . .' I do not recognize this voice."

"It is Emily's," she said calmly, though her eyes shone with elation.

"No." I could not believe it. How could Emily—this, this *cipher*—produce such lines of supernal power? "Compared to her, Elizabeth Barrett is minor!"

"It is so unlike poetry ever written by a woman."

"Woman? Might as well say *anyone!*"

Charlotte and I stood motionless, stunned into inaction.

"I did not know that she wrote!" I burst out.

"We all do," Charlotte answered.

"Forgive my presumption, but I have an idea—"

"I believe I may have preempted you."

"EMILY!" we both called, summoning her from the kitchen. As usual, her dress was blotched by fingers of flour.

"Emily," Charlotte began, holding forth the tiny book.

"Where did you get that?" Emily hissed, snatching it back from her sister.

"Emily, these poems are truly singular. Reading them is like listening to faerie music!"

"You should not have perused that which is not yours!"

"I beg your pardon: I was unaware of the book's contents. But sister—" Charlotte's voice broke. "I know no woman that ever lived ever wrote such poetry before!"

"They are but simple rhymes—nothing more."

"You are mistaken," I said boldly. "These are verses forged by genius. Not the weak, verbose effusions we get from most these days."

"They have energy and clarity."

"If you say so," the poetess grumbled, looking anxious to return to her baking.

"WAIT!" Charlotte commanded. "I have a plan—"

"The last one put us in Brussels. And we have emerged with a *single* pupil."

"True," Charlotte said. "But hear me out, I beg you."

Emily crossed her arms, causing her long sleeves to droop.

"Your work *must be* seen. Keeping it to yourself is no mere caprice—it is utterly *criminal*."

"Arrest me then."

"Are you aware—does Anne write poetry? She has been so . . . close lately."

Emily hesitated. "Better to ask *her*."

We called for the youngest to come downstairs.

"What is it?" she asked in alarm, spotting our tense triumvirate.

"Do you have any poems, Anne?" Charlotte asked.

"Well, I—yes, a few."

"And are they any good?"

Anne blushed.

"Of course they are," said Emily. "Do you take her for a dunce?"

"Hear then my present plan: We compile our best—for I too have been guilty of poesy—then send them off to be published. *In a book!*"

"Who pays for this?" asked Emily, the family's stern treasurer.

"We do. We still have a bit of Aunt's legacy. To what better aim might it be purposed?"

"Investment, perhaps?"

"Bah! That is the way of safety! And I never knew *you* to shun risk."

Emily stared down at Charlotte. "I refuse to submit to this lunatic scheme."

"Yet we cannot proceed without you! You are the greatest of us by far."

Anne started to soften. "It might be all right, sister. A chance to have our voices heard?"

"No!" Emily spat.

The next day, when Charlotte approached her:

"NO."

The day following, when Charlotte made a third attempt:

"NO!"

And the fourth day, when Charlotte cornered her on a chair, looking like a lancer about to charge:

"Very well then! If you feel these rhymes merit a book, so be it. *Just leave me alone.*"

Thus began production on what was to be the Brontës' first publication. Charlotte, fired with ambition, put heartbreak aside as she wrote to numerous publishers. None bothered to respond, but she would as soon surrender as Nelson. Finally, she asked advice from a firm that published encyclopedias (surely *they* would know), and they in turn directed her to Aylott and Jones of London.

By January, 1846, these gentlemen had agreed to publish the volume, at the not inconsiderable cost of thirty-one pounds, ten shillings.

I watched, thrilled, as the creation of the book took shape. Each sister would contribute a number of poems, and they worked all winter editing (in Emily's case, purging all mention of Gondal, her shared world with Anne). Most of Anne's poems had been written at Thorp Greene; most of Charlotte's, much earlier.

When I read "A Reminiscence" by Anne:

> Yes, thou art gone! and never more
> Thy sunny smile shall gladden me;
> But I may pass the old church door,
> And pace the floor that covers thee,
>
> May stand upon the cold, damp stone,
> And think that, frozen, lies below
> The lightest heart that I have known,
> The kindest I shall ever know.
>
> Yet, though I cannot see thee more,
> 'Tis still a comfort to have seen;
> And though thy transient life is o'er,
> 'Tis sweet to think that thou hast been;
>
> To think a soul so near divine,
> Within a form so angel fair,
> United to a heart like thine,
> Has gladdened once our humble sphere.

I thought at once of that handsome young man: the one depicted in her drawing. Had *Anne* been in love? Had the object died tragically young? It certainly seemed so from her poetry . . .

By contrast, Charlotte's lines were hardly a mystery, as in the opening to her (appropriately titled) "Passion":

> Some have won a wild delight,
> By daring wilder sorrow;
> Could I gain thy love to-night,
> I'd hazard death to-morrow.

Oddly, it was *Emily* who wrote best on love, something I was sure she had never experienced—in this world. *So much the better for her*, I thought, for exciting as the project was, I longed all the while for Branwell. Reader, I beg you—do not think he had been forgotten! Nor by his sisters, neither.

During the course of the book's assembly, Charlotte seemed stricken by guilt. "Do you think," she asked the others, "we should include Branwell? He was after all our first poet."

Anne thought hard. "We best not. A distraction at the present might prove a disaster."

"Agreed," said Emily. No wonder Ellen called them "twins." "We do not wish to cause a return to his sorry state. If he feels his work inferior, that might well be the result."

Charlotte nodded sadly. I did not like his exclusion but remained close as a stone, so as not to expose us both. Still, I was made of flesh and his slight caused me great sorrow

In February, the sisters finished their editing. All of the poems had been neatly copied and were ready to be sent off. But—true to form—Emily rebelled.

"Charlotte, Anne and I have determined that we want to publish under pseudonyms."

Charlotte started. "Whatever is the point of *that*?"

"We wish to continue our lives as they are."

"Do you not seek fame, Emily?"

"No. It is *you* who have sought it for me."

Charlotte sighed. A life of quietude was not for her, but she must respect her coauthors' wishes. "What did you have in mind?"

Anne said, "You are acquainted with Father's new curate, Mr. Bell Nicholls?"

"Unfortunately."

"What if we call ourselves 'the Bells'? I am to be Acton; Emily is Ellis; who do you wish to be? It must commence, naturally, with 'C.'"

Charlotte thought for a moment. "Let me be 'Currer Bell.'"

"Excellent!" Anne clapped her hands.

The fair copy was shipped to London, with the proof arriving in March. At long last, *Poems By Currer, Ellis, and Action Bell* was published in May 1846. Some of the notices were gratifying—in July, Sydney Dobell wrote for the *Athenaeum*:

> A fine quaint spirit has the latter [Ellis] which may have things to speak that men will be glad to hear and an evident power of wing that may reach heights not here attempted.

And,

> Here is a family in whom appears to run the instinct of song.

The sole disappointment arose at the dirty hands of Commerce: out of a thousand-copy print run, only two books were sold. But at least one of the purchasers requested the Bells' signatures!

To my mind, Emily and Anne were unmoved by their status as published authors. To Charlotte, however, this was a welcome lifeline for a fallen mountaineer. Once back atop the face, she boldly continued climbing. She possessed, in full measure, the Resolve that sometimes meets Luck and breeds that rare child Success.

A WOODLAND SPRITE

Reader, I beg your indulgence as I turn back to 1845, when the Parsonage buzzed with industry. Against my unexpressed wishes, Father demanded my presence for the Christmas holidays.

That year, they were held at his country estate: Briarwood, in West Sussex. I endured the train ride to London as well as *another* to Worthing, whose station appeared pristine, for it was but recently built. At last, I crawled into Father's carriage and made my way to his proudest possession.

Despite its prickly appellation, Briarwood was lovely. It had been in the family for centuries, and descended from the reign of Elizabeth, so there was many a domed turret and door with silver ironwork. In light of its Shelby ownership, it was of course ostentatious, but the grounds themselves were natural, encompassing rich timber forests. I was so fatigued by the time I arrived that I barely mouthed hello before tumbling into bed.

The next morning found me brighter with rest. I greeted my whole family and endeavored to embrace Isabelle. She was, she assured me, practically engaged to Lord Kirby. Father's Mrs. P——, attired in a red and green frock, was also in attendance, which I found rather repellent. It appeared this hardworking widow might well be the next Lady Shelby, a prospect I could not relish.

I confess I missed the Parsonage and all of my friends within: the sisters busily editing their *Poems*; even old Tabby slipping me a piece of pie. I dared not dwell on the inmate at Bradford, for then I should be miserable as Charlotte, and cast gloom across the whole company.

Christmas came and went—along with a plenitude of gifts, few of which could be useful at Haworth; I danced first with Colin then Alfred, but fear I was somewhat distant. I saw Father observing my movements: to be sure, his dreaded lecture arrived on schedule: the morning of Boxing Day.

"Well now," Father inquired, as we sat at the breakfast table. "Which young man shall it be? The handsome or the rich one? In my view, either is suitable, though the richer would be my preference."

"Please, Sir."

"Come, away with this false modesty! You are nearing twenty—high time to engage with *some* swain or other."

Emma giggled, dousing her waffles with syrup.

"I've not yet decided, Sir. I am sure the answer will come in the fullness of time."

"Humph! See to it that you do not apply too much thought. Else I'll accuse those Brontës of making you ineligible."

"Yes, Sir." In truth, I felt very low. I witnessed George and Athena still lost in the first glow of love, which made me even more desolate. I remained indoors for several days, listening to Emma chatter, but finally donned a coat and boots and ventured into the garden.

This was a tamed affair, as orderly as Kew Gardens. Every tree and shrub was manicured, along with a lawn of green perfection. To me, the weather was temperate after my sojourn in Haworth. In fact, there was no snow: just occasional ice on the path. I walked on, past the conquered landscape, into a copse of natural trees. I started to breathe freely as denuded branches enclosed me. The only sounds were my boots on the hard winter path and the distant bleating of sheep.

"Happy Christmas!" a voice sounded, and a lithe form leapt from an overturned log. My screams were dampened in the woodland setting, but that did not lessen my terror.

"Shhh, shhh!" said the unworldly being, bestowing a kiss on my cheek. "It is only I—Branwell. Not the King of the Faeries."

I pushed him away. "I nearly fell dead from fright!" The blood pumped quick in my ears. "However did you get here?"

"Same as you: via rail. Charlotte told me where you had gone. I sold a Christmas piece, purchased my ticket, and landed here." He spread his arms wide.

"How did you get from Worthing? Don't tell me—"

"I—you—WALKED!" we said together.

"It is but ten miles."

Staring at him, I shook my head. "I think you *must* have a drop of Faerie blood."

"As a half Irishman, I thank you." He bowed.

I looked around furtively. "It is not safe for you to be here. We must *not* be spied together!"

"Your instructions were never to visit the Parsonage, and you must confess that I have kept my word. This, however, is Sussex."

"I well know where we are! If Father discovers you here, he will surely call out his dogs."

"I fear neither man nor beast," Branwell said, straightening. "As long as I have you in my arms."

He stepped forward, and I felt that same strange tingle as he first embraced me, then showered me with kisses.

"Stop, stop! This accomplishes nothing."

He let me loose with surprise. "You sound as resolute as Charlotte."

"I wish I were, for—"

I hesitated, wondering if I should speak. It might drive him back to despair; but I felt he was part of the family and had a right to know.

"Your sisters are publishing a book. Of poems."

"And they did not ask me." He looked down at the thinly iced path.

"I know they considered you occupied—with your painting."

"Oh, I am occupied all right: by failure." He leant against a nearby horse chestnut. "I do not have the talent—nor the salesman's fervor—to become another Leyland. For the whole of this year, I have sold . . . two portraits. Hardly an incitement for your father to approve me."

"We could run away!"

"What?"

The thought had occurred to me sporadically, but for the first time I voiced it aloud. "To Brussels! To Paris! *Anywhere.*"

Branwell looked at me ruefully. "Once I would have embraced such a notion and been off with you directly. But now . . . one cannot live on nothing a year. Not even Becky Sharp."

I laughed at his *Vanity Fair* allusion.

"In truth—I cannot do it to *you. You* are unused to poverty: the harshness of the landlord at the door; the sheriff coming round to collect, lest he hurl you in jail. My Maria was not meant for that life, and I will not subject you to it."

"But I love you!" I cried. How was it that we had changed roles, with *myself* playing a Brontë?

"Trust me—I return that love, more than you can imagine. Without you, my world is perpetual night."

"Why must *money* separate us?"

"Because we live in the Age of Industry. Contrary to romantic novels, sometimes love is *not* enough."

We stood silent, a slight breeze ruffling bare branches.

"I have no fortune to call my own. Only what Father dispenses."

He nodded.

"Is there no way out of this labyrinth?"

"We must act the part of Theseus."

I wiped away my tears.

"Your account of my sisters' endeavor has served to raise my hopes. If the three of them can publish, what is there to prevent *me*?"

"Nothing," I said firmly.

"I have the skeleton of a novel. Something begun in a distant age and requiring much revision. It is but an unformed newborn; yet I believe that I can sculpt it so it takes the form of a man."

He seemed more filled with confidence than Theseus himself.

"*That* is a brilliant plan. Yet how will you live while you work?"

He sighed. "I fear that is the obstacle. In conscience— be amazed, for I *do* have one, at least while sober—I cannot ask Father for a single shilling more."

We both stood and considered that mistress called Fortune: one of us rich, though not until marriage; the other deficient in gold, but very rich in promise.

"Wait." An image had entered my mind. "Father has a small hunting cabin, not fifteen miles hence. It is usually stocked with provisions that might last a man a half year. No one ever goes there. Father is far too corpulent, and

George wielding a gun is as frightful a prospect as *you* with one."

"Hmmm." Branwell seemed to be weighing this seriously. "If I require more time to finish, I can seek local employment."

"Just so!" We fed on each other's delight like two guests at a banquet. "Do you have your novel at hand?"

"No, but no matter—I will simply begin anew. What there was is essentially . . . detritus."

"Meet me at this same spot in two hours, and I will supply a profusion of paper, pens, and ink. Such items will never be missed—by the Shelbys."

I purloined as much as I could from Father's desk, and also visited my room. I paced with impatience until the clock struck four.

I heard him whistling before I saw him by the old horse chestnut. I pressed into his hands my meager pocket money, along with a large box containing a writer's tools. I had also drawn for him a crude, penciled map.

"Best of luck," I told him. "I *know* that you can do it!"

"With you behind me, how can I fail?"

He kissed me deeply, then trotted off into the dim winter light.

"I return a renowned man of letters!" he called, his voice rebounding through trees.

I smiled into the gloom. This was the old Branwell—filled with self-assurance—prior to his downfall in York. Now, his cup overflowing with Exuberance, he also had the strong draught Reason to serve as her guide.

THREE MASTERPIECES

My return to Haworth was a happy one, since my knowledge of a fourth writing Brontë buoyed my hopes for the future. I must confess that I told a little white lie: informing all the Parsonage that I'd met Branwell in London, and he had told *me* he was going to Paris to further his study of art. I fear I also let slip that recent commissions financed the journey . . .

However, the three Brontë sisters were also guilty of subterfuge. It so happened that the book of poems was *not* their sole industry. Since the discovery of Emily's verses, there was another—far weightier—disclosure in store. Unbeknownst to Charlotte, they were all setting down words in a far lengthier form: for each had begun a novel!

Anne preceded the others and was nearly two-thirds through. Her sisters lagged by some months—though Emily's book would not boast "The End" until the following June.

With clandestineness lifted, the salon became a sun fueled by partnership. After Mr. Brontë retired at nine, Charlotte, Emily, and Anne would converge on the small space, pacing round the table, as they had in their youth (Ellen reported that in those days, Charlotte even performed an occasional pirouette!).

At present, expensive candles were extinguished, the only light supplied by the moon and a small grated fire. Yet even Nyx, goddess of night, could not halt the Illumination coming from these three minds.

I never joined the procession: I felt I was not deserving. But I *did* sprawl on the sofa, listening to and witnessing the birth of three masterpieces!

"Anne, you are wrong to halt your story and preach obvious truths. Is Agnes a governess or a vicar?"

"Emily, such Truths are the reason I write. And *must you* be so brutal—so coarse—through every page of *Wuthering Heights*?"

Emily gave a delighted laugh. "Listen to this—it's when Lockwood runs into Heathcliff.

> "I hope it will be a lesson to you to make no more rash journeys on these hills," cried Heathcliff's stern voice from the kitchen entrance. "As to staying here, I don't keep accommodations for visitors: you must share a bed with Hareton or Joseph, if you do."
>
> "I can sleep on a chair in this room," I replied.
>
> "No, no! A stranger is a stranger, be he rich or poor: it will not suit me to permit any one the range of the place while I am off guard!" said the unmannerly wretch.
>
> With this insult my patience was at an end. I uttered an expression of disgust, and pushed past him into the yard, running against Earnshaw in my haste. It was so dark that I could not see the means of exit; and, as I wandered round, I heard another specimen of their civil behaviour amongst each other. At first the young man appeared about to befriend me.
>
> "I'll go with him as far as the park," he said.
>
> "You'll go with him to hell!" exclaimed his master, or whatever relation he bore. "And who is to look after the horses, eh?"

"A man's life is of more consequence than one evening's neglect of the horses: somebody must go," murmured Mrs. Heathcliff, more kindly than I expected.

"Not at your command!" retorted Hareton. "If you set store on him, you'd better be quiet."

"Then I hope his ghost will haunt you; and I hope Mr. Heathcliff will never get another tenant till the Grange is a ruin," she answered, sharply.

"Hearken, hearken, shoo's cursing on 'em!" muttered Joseph, toward whom I had been steering.

"Emily!" Charlotte cried, "you cannot spell out 'h-e-l-l.'"

"I'll be damned if I can't! And I will."

Charlotte closed her eyes.

"Emily, really, must the text burst with blood, a knife forced between Nellie's teeth, and constant threats of whipping?" Anne shivered.

Emily chuckled. "Of course! It is a Gondal story."

"Oftentimes I wish we had not written as children." Charlotte shook her head. However, she cheered considerably when Anne read from her own *Agnes Grey*, or *Passages in the Life of An Individual.*

All true histories contain instruction; though, in some, the treasure may be hard to find, and when found, so trivial in quantity, that the dry, shriveled kernel scarcely compensates for the trouble of cracking the nut. Whether this be the case with my history or not, I am hardly competent to judge. I sometimes think it might prove useful to some, and entertaining to others; but the world may judge for itself. Shielded by my own obscurity, and by the lapse of years, and a few fictitious names, I do not fear to venture; and will candidly lay before the public what I would not disclose to the most intimate friend.

"*That* is more like it! Emily, do consider the popular taste. Recall that our goal is publication—not excommunication!"

"Popular taste be damned! This is *my* world, and I shall people it as I please."

"Thank the Lord it is only in her head," Anne whispered to Charlotte.

"I believe that is the aspect which frightens me most."

"No whispering! Let us hear from Charlotte now."

Charlotte read a brief passage from her *The Professor*. As I listened to this tale told in a male's voice, I came to an unsought conclusion: this book was sorely lacking. Since Miss Brontë was my favorite, I confess this greatly upset me. As George Eliot might go on to state: it is crushing when our idols disappoint us.

Still, Emily's readings kept me on edge as I awaited ensuing chapters. Whatever Charlotte's and Anne's objections, one could never accuse *Wuthering Heights* of dullness!

The procession of the sisters round the table ended in early July 1846. Charlotte completed the fair copy of her book, and immediately wrote to a publisher. After numerous rejections (which Charlotte did not conceal, for she submitted the same envelope with the previous names crossed out) a London house—Newby—agreed to publish Anne and Emily. But *not* Charlotte's *Professor*.

Even as I write this so many years later, I confess I find it fabulous that the author of *Wuthering Heights* paid fifty pounds for its production! Yet I assure you it was so.

I cannot record firsthand Charlotte's reaction to her first rejection. She was far away in Manchester, serving as Mr. Brontë's companion while he had surgery on his eyes. What she accomplished there would soon open the collective ones of the world.

A Book of Decided Power

I heard afterward that upon receiving that rejection, Charlotte began a new novel that very day. Mr. Brontë's surgery was successful; Dr. Wilson skillfully removed his cataracts, and it was hoped that his vision would now be much improved.

In the meantime, he was to recuperate in near darkness, as Charlotte sat by his room, forbidden even to speak to him. While a nurse looked to his care and Charlotte suffered mightily from toothache, she put pen to paper. Over the course of the next five weeks, she wrote nonstop, in the grip of her old muse.

When she and her father returned to Haworth, he did seem a changed man. He was able to read and write on his own, which was a great relief to Emily. Now he could even walk without being led.

The sisters' nighttime procession restarted as Charlotte debuted her latest. This was the first passage she read aloud, from a penciled, little square book. It is Jane in the garden at Thornfield.

> Sweet-briar and southernwood, jasmine, pink, and rose have long been yielding their evening sacrifice of incense: this new scent is neither of shrub nor flower; it is—I know it well—it is Mr. Rochester's cigar. I look round and I listen. I see trees laden with ripening fruit. I hear a nightingale

warbling in a wood half a mile off; no moving form is visible, no coming step audible; but that perfume increases: I must flee. I make for the wicket leading to the shrubbery, and I see Mr. Rochester entering. I step aside into the ivy recess; he will not stay long: he will soon return whence he came, and if I sit still he will never see me.

We were all enrapt, even the stoic Emily. Then came the Proposal scene.

> "I tell you I must go!" I retorted, roused to something like passion. "Do you think I can stay to become nothing to you? Do you think I am an automaton?—a machine without feelings? And can bear to have my morsel of bread snatched from my lips, and my drop of living water dashed from my cup? Do you think, because I am poor, obscure, plain, and little, I am soulless and heartless? You think wrong!—I have as much soul as you—and full as much heart! And if God had gifted me with some beauty and much wealth, I should have made it as hard for you to leave me, as it is now for me to leave you. I am not talking to you now through the medium of custom, conventionalities, nor even of mortal flesh;—it is my spirit that addresses your spirit; just as if both had passed through the grave, and we stood at God's feet, equal,—as we are!"

Charlotte's fierce declamation ended. Anne stood wide-eyed, while Emily went pale. I said the first thing that came to mind: "Miss Brontë, let me kiss you!"

I walked over to her small form and delivered a peck on her cheek. Anne and Emily did likewise, all of us bending considerably.

"That is more like it," said Emily.

"Charlotte—that is the best you have ever done!" Anne's blue eyes sparkled.

"Miss Brontë," I said, "this calls for a toast!"

I strode across the hall, into her father's study, removing a bottle of claret and four rather small glasses. I walked back with energy, filling each glass to the brim.

"To *Jane Eyre*," I proclaimed, raising my crystal high.

"To Currer Bell," said Emily and Anne, clinking along with me. The Great Ride had just begun.

The publication of *Jane Eyre* unfolded like a fairy story: a reader at Smith, Elder and Co., Mr. Williams, had sent Charlotte a hopeful note about *The Professor*, requesting to see her next. To his amazement, she shipped the new manuscript on 24 August 1847—*a mere two weeks later*.

Once Williams received it and started to read, he realized he could not stop. He begged his publisher, George Smith, to peruse the book post-haste. Smith was skeptical, but when he opened the book on a Sunday, he found he could not put it down.

This was a common effect—even on the great Thackeray, who wrote Williams: "I wish you had not sent me *Jane Eyre*. It interested me so much that I have lost (or won if you like) a whole day in reading it . . . . some of the love passages made me cry, to the astonishment of John, who came in with the coals . . . . I don't know why I tell you this but that I have been exceedingly moved and pleased .... It is a woman's writing, but whose?"

Charlotte learned within a fortnight that Smith, Elder would publish the book—and recompense her one hundred pounds (later upped to five hundred). For Charlotte—who had earned sixteen pounds per annum as a governess—this was no less than a fortune. A mere six weeks later, on 16 October 1847, *Jane Eyre* was released to England. Twenty-five hundred copies were printed and sold out in three short months.

Initial acclaim for "Currer Bell" graced all the literary magazines.

> *Jane Eyre* is a book of decided power. (*The Examiner*)

> It *is* an autobiography—not, perhaps, in the naked facts and circumstances, but in the actual suffering and experience. . . . [I]t is soul speaking to soul: it is an utterance from the depths of a struggling, suffering, much enduring spirit. (G.H. Lewes, *Fraser's Magazine*)

> This is an extraordinary book. Although a work of fiction, it is no mere novel, for there is nothing but Nature & Truth about it. . . .for power of thought and expression we do not know its rival among modern productions. All the serious novel writers of the day lose in comparison with Currer Bell . . . . (*Era*)

After Smith spread the word in London that Thackeray had *personally* written to the author, *Jane Eyre* was declared "the best novel of the season."

I watched this maelstrom strike the Parsonage from my lookout's perch on the mast. With each packet of glowing reviews (forwarded by Williams), Charlotte entered further into the realm of disbelief. At last, she was where she wanted to be, when she had written Southey in 1837 and he had responded: "Literature cannot be the business of a woman's life, and it ought not to be." Still, she had persevered. Through teaching, through governessing, and heartache, she never lost sight of her early ambition. Without Charlotte, there would be no (known) *Wuthering Heights*; no virtuosic *Tenant of Wildfell Hall. She* was the Engine—fueled not by steam but resolve—who propelled the writing Bells out of village obscurity.

Those first days were heady indeed. While Anne and Emily struggled with Newby and his error-laden proofs, Charlotte (or, rather, *Currer Bell*) received acclaim as the great new author of the day—in a decade that boasted not only Thackeray, but Dickens.

On the first of October, she received six bound copies from Smith to dispense to whom she liked. She kept one for herself, gifted one each to Emily, Anne, and Mr. Brontë, and saved a set for Branwell. I was shocked to discover that the sixth was reserved for *me* and not for Mary Taylor!

"I—I don't know what to say, Miss Brontë." I choked between tears. "This is the most wonderful present ever."

Charlotte smiled and gave me a hug as she passed. Her arms could reach only around my midsection. I opened the book to its frontispiece—saw the neat handwriting that was so familiar.

1 October 1847

My Dearest Maria,

To my <u>favorite</u> pupil and the woman I am proud to call Friend. Though you have made remarkable progress, you have many years before you—<u>never stop learning or creating</u>.

Love,

CB (you know what it actually stands for)

Reader, I do not believe I was ever so moved in my life. To be deemed "Friend" to this extraordinary woman—to have the privilege of knowing her and to have witnessed the birth of one of the world's great novels—it was all too much to bear.

I sobbed into my handkerchief, taking care not to drench my gift. As I sit in my study now, if I incline my head but slightly, I can see its modest binding: a little worse for wear, but by the same token, so am I.

No material good can take its place, for simply *to look on the book* fills me with exquisite joy. Indeed, I would not trade that plain cloth copy for all the riches on earth.

"CONVENTIONALITY IS NOT MORALITY"

Alas, Charlotte's reign as the petted darling of London lasted no longer than her general happiness. As she herself would write: "I concluded it to be a part of His great plan that some must deeply suffer while they live, and I thrilled in the certainty that of this number, I was one."[10]

It was not that *Jane Eyre* ceased to be popular—far from it—but the book's "scandalous" declarations—that women were *equal* to men and that Jane had every right to marry her social superior—sent chills up the Victorian spine.

First, there was the ludicrous review in *The Mirror*, stating that the author "overstep[s] conventional usages" and "trample[s] upon customs established by our forefathers."

Then came *The Economist*, which praised the book if written by a man, but pronounced it "odious" if written by a woman.

Later notices were even worse, such as Elizabeth Rigby's in *The Quarterly Review*. She decried the book's "coarseness of taste" and "heathenish doctrine of religion," and claims it is a dangerous picture of "a natural heart." In her view, this tale of a plain governess might lead to the actual Apocalypse, for the novel is

---

[10] *Villette*

accused of being "pre-eminently an anti-Christian composition," and is guilty of "a murmuring against the comforts of the rich and against the privations of the poor, which, as far as each individual is concerned, is a murmuring against God's appointment." The prevailing tone, one of "ungodly discontent," allies *Jane Eyre* in Miss Rigby's view to the cast of mind and thought "which has overthrown authority and violated every code human and divine abroad, and fostered Chartism and rebellion at home."

When Williams sent on this screed in December 1848, I laughed until the tears came. Charlotte, with her Tory politics, accused of being a Radical! She herself was stunned. When she read that she was anti-religion, she cried, "But I love the Church of England!" She could not comprehend how these critics had twisted her words: when Jane leaves Rochester, it is *because* she will not violate her own conscience—which directly reflects the precepts of the Church!

"To hell with them," Emily told her.

"They are being horribly unfair," said Anne.

"Miss Brontë, do not distress yourself—*Jane Eyre* will live after these fools are dust."

Still Charlotte, being Charlotte, was deeply hurt. She launched back at her critics in the preface to the second edition.

> Conventionality is not morality. Self-righteousness is not religion. To attack the first is not to assail the last. To pluck the mask from the face of the Pharisee, is not to lift an impious hand to the Crown of Thorns.

I must confess, I loved her feisty spirit. I did not enjoy seeing her upset, but knew—after witnessing her trials—that she would outlast the bigots. She *would* tell the Truth and, as Emily said, let the critics be damned!

In the meantime, she and Anne continued their struggles with Newby. He stalled continually before releasing the Bell books in December 1847. The authors were horrified, as all their meticulous proofing was absent.

"I shall kill him!" Emily raged. But her enemies hewed her down first.

If *Jane Eyre* was considered coarse, it was *nothing* to *Wuthering Heights*. The author was informed that the "general effect is inexpressibly painful"; her characters are "thoroughly hateful or utterly contemptible. If you do not detest the person, you despise him; and if you do not despise him, you detest him with all your heart." "It strongly shows the brutalizing influence of unchecked passion."

There were a few who understood her, as with the American critic George Washington Peck.

> If the rank of a work of fiction is to depend solely on its naked imaginative power, then this is one of the greatest novels in the language.

Emily, unlike Charlotte, showed no signs of duress, nor did she attempt a defense. She continued her daily duties as if nothing were amiss. We would discover—all too soon—that the reviews wounded her deeply.

On a wintry day after I had scribbled some French, I walked down to a familiar spot. This was a waterfall dubbed by the Brontës "The Meeting of the Waters." It was in a valley with outcrops of boulders that seemed strewn by a giant's hand. The waterfall itself was composed of tiered rocks down which the liquid—of varying intensity—flowed. Now, in the thick of winter, the result was a mere trickle.

I was not unduly surprised to find Emily seated there. This was a favorite haunt, and she perched at the edge of the stones, oblivious to cold and snow.

"Hello, Miss Emily," I said. She inclined her head slightly. She was so dependably obscure that I had no hint as to her mood. Still, I decided to mount my charge.

"Miss Emily, I think the critics are wrong—horribly wrong—in their assessment of *Wuthering Heights*. Cannot they see the beauty and force? The wild depictions of Nature that do not waste a word, yet transport us to these very moors?"

"It is not really Yorkshire—"

"I know. But you pretend that it is. And that last line: 'I ... wondered how anyone could ever imagine unquiet slumbers for the sleepers in that quiet earth.' I shall remember it the whole of my life!"

She relinquished a small smile.

"Is it true? Will Cathy and Heathcliff be happy, now that they're united in death?"

"*I* like to think so."

I let out a frosty breath. "Do you know what I think?"

"How could I, since your thoughts are constrained in your head?"

"I think you are *beyond* critics. When I reflect on the dolts I know in London, it is not so much a wonder that they scorn the book, but rather that they can read at all!"

She laughed.

"I just wanted to tell you to your face: you are one of the greatest writers the world has ever seen. Your words will live forever."

For the first time in nearly four years, I saw her eyes dampen with moisture.

"Thank you."

"Thank *you*," I said, before scrambling off and leaving her a solitary, which I knew she most desired.

Poor Anne made the least impact on reviewers—her book was nearly ignored—and *The Atlas* said that *Agnes Grey* is a "coarse imitation of one of Miss Austen's charming stories. . . . It leaves no painful impression on the mind—some may think it leaves no impression at all."

Absurd. In my now-enlightened view (as a pupil taught by three geniuses), this was a patent untruth. *Agnes* is in fact charming and wise, often reaching the skill of Miss Austen. I meant to tell Anne as much at the first opportunity. We were about to commence geography.

"Let us discuss the formation of the earth."

"Miss Anne—"

"Yes?"

"Those *Atlas* fools need an Atlas! I *loved* Agnes Grey: she has such a subtle humor, and when she encounters

Mr. Weston on the sand, well . . . it was so romantic, I cried!"

"Really?"

"Of course. It is only that this book is *quieter* than the other Bells'—certainly not inferior."

"Well. I thank you. Yes, very much." She was so unassuming that her pale cheeks deepened with red, but I could tell she was not unmoved. In fact, when she strode past me to fetch a map, she kissed the top of my head!

As if reviews were not bad enough, there still existed a Newby. He seemingly had one last trick up his unscrupulous sleeve. He intimated strongly to the public that the great Currer Bell had produced a second novel: none other than *Wuthering Heights!*

A letter flew from Smith to Charlotte, inquiring as to why *he* had not first rights to her latest work?

That was all that Charlotte required: She would *not* sit quiet in Haworth while being accused of calumny. Her sharp mind evolved a new scheme, this one requiring activity: in order to prove that the Bells were three separate people, to London they would go.

"We Are Three Sisters"

Just prior to departure, there was an altercation, spearheaded (as always) by Emily. Charlotte called to her from the dining room.

"Emily! Why do you tarry? We must set Smith, Elder to rights with all possible haste."

Emily stood in her father's study. "*I* am not going anywhere."

"But you should," Charlotte pleaded. "We must prove beyond a doubt that there exists a trio of Bells—not merely a Currer."

"I am wholly uninterested."

"But Emily," Anne said gently, "they are assigning your authorship to Charlotte."

"The Devil take them!" she spat. "What do I care?"

It was impossible—not by any worldly being, as M. Heger would affirm—to change Emily's mind. She was as unresponsive as a statue. Charlotte and Anne began to despair.

"Wait," I said, for the nucleus of a plan had entered my scheming head.

The sisters all stared at me.

"What if *I* become Ellis Bell? No one in London knows 'him,' and it is assured that *I* know no one in publishing."

Emily grinned.

"We should not lie," Anne fretted. "*That* is always wrong."

"Yet Newby *is* abominably wrong to pass off Ellis's work as mine!" Charlotte started to pace. I knew she had other concerns regarding the attribution: *Wuthering Heights* was simply too wild for her.

Now she looked at me. "Do you truly believe you can do this?"

"Of course. I merely stare into the distance, pretending to look mystical. I dress in ancient raiment, and insult all who come near."

Emily roared with laughter. Even Anne smiled.

"Well . . ." Charlotte was the Leader, and it was her distinct province to pronounce yea or nay.

"All right. We may certainly make the attempt. If Maria cannot pass as Ellis, we confess to Mr. Smith."

"Excellent," said Emily. "Let me know if she makes a credible me."

Charlotte and Anne rushed upstairs, while Emily beckoned to me. "Remember," she advised, "if anyone asks why you do as you do, simply respond, 'I wish to be as God made me.'"

I solemnly mouthed the phrase. "Thank you!" I too ran upstairs to pack my smallest bag.

This particular journey to Keighley I shall never forget. It was 7 July 1848. We practically *ran* through a storm—over steep hills—to arrive! By this time, a railway station had been built, enabling us to travel direct to London.

I suggested to Charlotte and Anne that they stay with me at Harley Street, but they would hear none of it. They wished to lodge at a strange inn (for single women, at least) in Paternoster Row: The Chapter Coffee House. This is where the Brontës had stayed ere their departure to Brussels. One could see Saint Paul's mighty dome through the window, a sight that particularly thrilled Charlotte. Anne, who had never been to the great town, seemed overwhelmed by its sights: her hands revealed a slight tremble.

We arrived at Paternoster Row by eight o'clock the next morning. Charlotte rushed us through breakfast, for we must make our way to Smith, Elder. I made the attempt to dress as plainly as my companions, yet stood out like an imposter. *My* frocks were far from homemade.

Thus began my debut as Ellis. We arrived at the great publishing house at 65 Cornhill Row. In the vestibule, Charlotte requested that a clerk retrieve Mr. Smith. Within minutes, the nervous young man reappeared.

"He wishes to know your names."

As always, Charlotte took command. "I fear they cannot be revealed. We have come to see him on a private matter."

The clerk looked truly frightened, then reluctantly retraced his steps. He emerged with a handsome young man—twenty-five or so—who stared at us in amazement. Why were three country bumpkins troubling him on a Saturday?

Wordlessly, Charlotte handed over an envelope addressed to "Currer Bell, Esq." The seal had clearly been broken.

"Where did you obtain this?" Smith asked sharply.

"From the post!" Charlotte crowed. "We have come that you might have ocular proof—there are *three of us!*"

Smith looked down at the letter, then again at us. It appeared he might fall over. Charlotte gave a laugh.

"Good God! Forgive me, ladies—I must tell Lewes and Thackeray—if they knew that Currer Bell was in town, they would have to be shut up!" He started to move forward, then back, like a madman.

"I thank you, Mr. Smith," said Charlotte, "but we wish to remain obscure. As much as I long to meet Thackeray, it will prove easier for us at home."

Smith made a disappointed face.

"I beg your pardon: this is Acton—and Ellis. We are three sisters!"

Anne gave a small curtsy. "How do you do?" she asked shyly.

In best Ellis fashion, I grunted and turned away.

We were introduced to Mr. Williams, the man to whom Charlotte effectively owed her career. With great emotion, the two shook hands. As Anne teared up, I made sure to roll my eyes.

"Please," said Smith. "You must be my guest at Bayswater for the duration of your visit—how my mother and sisters would relish hosting the Bells!"

"Alas, we wish to remain unknown even to your relations. And we are comfortably ensconced in our own lodgings at present."

In my persona of Ellis, I wanted to grab Charlotte and shake her! She was refusing every gift: the chance of creature comfort; of being lionized by a city that adored her. All this, merely to cater to Emily! I gave a low moan.

"Is Mr. Ellis well?" Smith asked solicitously.

"You must ignore my sister Emily. She does not care for society."

I decided to seize the moment and demonstrate. *"Might we at least sit down?"* I cried.

"Of course. How thoroughly rude of me." Smith had his clerk pull up three chairs as Charlotte shot me a warning glance. Yet I thought I was playing my role with lifelike exactitude!

Mr. Smith conveyed that he wished to take us out that evening. In the interim, we found a modest shop where I cheerfully bought gloves for my "sisters."

"Miss Brontë and Miss Anne, I beg you—allow me to purchase for you two fancy evening dresses. You will be the cream of London fashion!"

"No, no," Anne demurred.

"I think not, though your generosity is appreciated. We will be exactly as we are."

We returned to our odd lodging, where Charlotte—one of the world's great hypochondriacs—immediately fell ill with headache. The excitement of the morning was simply too much for her nerves.

When Smith appeared later, accompanied by his two sisters, they were spectacularly dressed in the finery of the season. For the first time in years, I longed for my old wardrobe. Yet this was not to be.

We rode in Smiths' carriage to that loftiest of amusements, the London Opera House. As we ascended the red-carpeted staircase, we passed by glittering notables. In contrast, we Bells looked like housemaids hired to dust the banister. I prayed I would not be recognized, but there was a fair probability I would be. With importune timing, I might even find myself facing Father or George! This thought made me as surly as the being I impersonated.

I saw two society matrons, in rich silk festooned with flowers, give us an incredulous look. One half-whispered to the other, "Who *is* that? Country cousins fresh from the field?" The other laughed. I walked over, looking them up and down.

"I wish to be as God made me," I said.

This seemed to freeze them. I slipped my arm into Anne's as we made our way to Smith's box, for I could see she was terrified. Charlotte coped well with the stares, even braving a small smile.

How I wished she had risen to announce: "Ladies and gentlemen, *I* am Currer Bell, author of *Jane Eyre*"—then witness their fawning. Those who treated her small, quaint form with contempt had no idea what lay behind those dark eyes—what majestic prose could flow free from her pen.

I hardly paid attention as *Barber of Seville* unfolded: I was far too occupied in shielding my own face. It was ironical, but *my* desire for obscurity nearly surpassed the Brontës'. As Rossini's soaring soprano dealt with all manner of trickery, I sat there reviewing my own.

That evening, I *almost* escaped detection, but while we waited for the carriage, a casual acquaintance approached.

"Maria Shelby!" she called. "Whatever are you doing in those clothes?"

"Surely you must mistake me." I smiled, drawing her away from my party. "Cecelia, in point of fact, I am rehearsing for a play."

"Really!"

"Yes, I and my fellow players have resolved to maintain our characters even off the stage."

"You—an *actress*?" She looked positively horrified.

"Not professional, no! This is a private entertainment. Pray do not spoil the fun and mention my appearance her."

"Of course." Cecelia ambled off, and I was able to breathe again. That meeting could well have resulted in catastrophe!

Our next few days in town were filled with a whirlwind of visits: to the Smiths'; to the Williamses'; even to the National Gallery. I discerned that Smith's family was puzzled by our identity. Yet they remained politely silent, even when *I* refused to speak. My fledging skill as an actress was put to the test again when Smith cornered me by a Titian.

"Excuse me, Ellis," he whispered. "I must ask about your creation—the marvelous *Wuthering Heights*."

Oh no, I thought.

"How did you first conceive the idea?"

I attempted to harness the spirit of Emily. "It came to me, that is all."

"And Mr. Heathcliff—is he based on someone you know?"

"Of course not! That is why it is called 'fiction.'" I rolled my eyes to the ceiling.

Smith would not be dissuaded. "And what would you say is the overall *meaning* of the work?"

"Name of God! Are we holding school in a gallery? I have *one* doltish pupil at present—I do not need another!" I heightened the effect of petulance by storming off in a huff. In truth, I had not the slightest idea of a moral to Emily's book.

Charlotte caught up with Smith.

"Rather prickly, is she not?"

"That is Emily," Charlotte shrugged.

Thanks be to Heaven, I was forced to maintain my charade only until the twelfth. That is when Charlotte and Anne—laden with books from Smith and Williams— boarded the train to Keighley.

I, however, remained behind. In yet another fabrication (this one devoid of costume), I claimed I was going to "visit family" in Sussex.

PROGRESS

I arrived at Worthing in good time, but hesitated at the small station. No private carriage awaited to speed me toward Father's estate. Since I was dressed in my "Emily best," I decided to summon some courage and hail the public coach.

Had Father (or George) known of my actions, the ornate roof of Briarwood might have come crashing down. Happily, I knew the family was in London, and had assiduously avoided contact so as not to risk a sighting.

Now, as I exited the coach at a crossroads (feeling much like Jane at Morton), I attempted to gauge my whereabouts. The foliage was thick with summer growth, yet I still retained a memory of a narrow forest path.

After walking "a mere ten miles," I spied distinctive grey turrets. However, that was not my destination. I turned away from the great house, diverging on another path. My light summer shoes crunched between oaks, and I was forced to halt on occasion due to enervating fatigue. *No true Brontë I!* The heavy satchel I bore did nothing to speed my progress. At last, after *four hours* of footsore travel, I spotted a small wooden hut peeking out from branching trees.

"Branwell!" I called. I saw no evidence of life, neither on four feet nor two. Looking about cautiously, I gratefully dropped my burden.

I saw a thick red mop rise by the lower corner of a window. Then, the door flung open, and *he* was beside me, taking me in his arms.

"Why have you not written these six months?" I kissed him full on the lips. God help me—I sounded identical to Charlotte!

He moved his head back from mine, running his hands through my hair. "You may trust I restrained the urge daily. But my sisters are wondrously clever and would have questioned the Worthing postmark."

"As for me, I could not address a letter to 'Sir Shelby's Lodge in the Forest.'"

"Alas, there is no rabbit post!"

I took a step back and examined his ragged clothing.

"This will never do. You have grown so thin. And wan."

"No more the consequence of spending a half year like a monk. With rather churchlike rations."

"Yes! I have brought you all my pin money—twenty pounds—so that you may purchase more from a shop."

"That pin must be as big as man," he remarked, as he gratefully pocketed the notes. "I thank you. You will be mentioned *first* in my book's acknowledgements." He gave me a peck on the cheek.

"Please! Not under my actual name. I have just spent half a fortnight pretending to be Emily."

He looked puzzled, and I related the story of the Bells, those "three brothers who are Lancashire weavers" — according to popular lore. I reached into my satchel and handed him its bounty: the sister's three published novels. He looked almost dumbstruck as he regarded them.

"Do you know, 'Currer Bell' is the toast of London! If Charlotte had chosen to reveal herself, she would have been swarmed by the likes of Thackeray."

Branwell's eyes went wide. He seized the first volume of *Jane Eyre*, opened to the front, and read several pages. At last, he closed the leaves.

"Brilliant," he said, nodding.

"You should see Emily's! It has frightened to death all of England. She and Charlotte have been accused of outright depravity."

He laughed. "They do not disappoint."

"Anne's book is lyric and lovely: the first real relation of what it is to be a governess."

"Dear Anne. I trust that all in Haworth are well?"

"Yes, including your father, whose vision has been restored. Oh, I have so much to tell you!"

He sat down on a tall fallen log, steering me into his lap. We remained thus, in utter quietude, for a few blessed moments.

"You must tell first!" I said finally. "How goes the fourth Bell's novel?"

"Henceforth, please address me as 'Bertram Bell.' The work goes well indeed. I have completed the first volume and am prepared to embark on the second."

"What is the general theme?"

"It is based on an Angrian story of mine—the world that 'Currer' and I created. I have titled it *And the Weary Are at Rest*. Happily, it is not as ghastly as the original."

"Excellent. I *told* you that you could do it!"

"Being here is a godsend—away from dissolute 'friends' and the public house. The sounds that assail me are merely the cheerful chirp of birds and insects. I must confess—I have grown to like the South, despite my Yorkshire breeding."

"I am glad. Someday perhaps we may have a house of our own in London."

"Not so grand as the Shelbys'!"

"That is unattainable. I mean: a proper *author's* house, with a profusion of libraries and books!"

"And Thackeray for dinner."

"We could invite your sisters and have them abandon their subterfuge. Though Emily, I fear, might well strike the great man."

We both laughed.

"You must be famished!" he exclaimed, entering the wood lodge and emerging with a plate of crackers and even some cooked meat. I looked at him.

"I have become a rather good hunter in my Green Man of the Forest guise."

I looked alarmed.

"Fear not—no boiled unicorn! It is simply rabbit."

I gratefully consumed the food, along with cups of fresh, clear water.

My epic journey from Worthing had left me not only footsore but weary. I noted that the sun now threatened to set, for it was nearly nine.

"Ah," said Branwell, "let us see about bedding you down for the night."

I reacted *exactly* as a young lady should. "Surely you do not anticipate that I will share your accommodation?"

"Unless you wish to sleep beneath an oak. It is nearly warm enough."

"No, no—I must be getting back. I should achieve London by daybreak and continue onto Keighley. I cannot abandon my studies when I have taken them thus far!"

Branwell smiled. "I hardly think the knowledge will seep from your head overnight."

"Still, it is . . ." I struggled for the words. "Highly inappropriate—scandalous—unthinkable!"

"As are my sister's books, or so you say."

"*We* are not words on a page—we are a young man and woman. Cossetted alone in the forest! If this report got abroad, it would taint me forever . . . consign to the crypt my future prospects for—"

"Marriage?" he asked. "Perhaps you do not recall that you are going to marry *me*." He slipped his arms around me.

"Of course I do," I said weakly. "Surely you must recognize—even as a Brontë and Green Man—that we *cannot* bed down together."

"You do not recollect the plan of your own property? This lodge was built for several hunters—therefore, it contains a number of beds."

I blushed. "Yes. I am very sorry to have doubted you."

He pushed me gently to my feet, and we walked inside the lodge, which smelled of fresh-cut flowers. He pointed to a small cot opposite his own. What happened that night, Reader, will remain as clandestine as the Bells' identity was. I will say only that it involved much kissing, a fair amount of hugging, and the repetition of the words "I love you" extensively from both parties.

It was therefore with much happiness that I endured the walk back to Worthing, train rides to London and Keighley, and eventual return to Haworth.

IN THE VALLEY OF THE SHADOW OF DEATH

Upon my arrival, all was well for six weeks. My lessons with the sisters resumed and Charlotte continued to work on *Shirley*, her next novel. Anne's latest, *The Tenant of Wildfell Hall*, was published by Newby in July 1848.

I read the latter eagerly, struck by Anne's frank treatment of drunkenness and debauchery.

I could not wait to ask her about it. One afternoon, as we reviewed theorems, I put forth one of my own: "Miss Anne, I trust I am acquainted with the model for your gentlemens' vices?"

She nodded.

"From where though did Helen Huntingdon emerge? It seems an amazing act for a wife to abandon her husband, since under our laws, she is his legal property."

"Yes." Anne pursed her lips. "Two years ago, a Mrs. Collins came to speak to Papa. She was the wife of a curate in Keighley: one who used her dreadfully. Papa recommended that she leave him—I understand she did not. I never had a chance to speak to her, since I was from home at the time."

"Your father is a brave man."

"He does what he feels is right. So must we all."

I nodded. Truly it stretched credulity that this shy, pious woman had written a book of such brutality. The critics' response was likewise.

> There is a coarseness of tone throughout the writings of all these Bells, that puts an offensive subject in its worst point of view. (*The Spectator*)

Happily, Anne achieved the final victory. Due to its titillating content, *The Tenant* became a best seller. A second edition was actually printed the following month, allowing Anne to have her say:

> My object in writing the following pages was not simply to amuse the Reader; neither was it to gratify my own taste, nor yet to ingratiate myself with the Press and the Public: I wished to tell the truth, for truth always conveys its own moral to those who are able to receive it. . . . Let it not be imagined, however, that I consider myself competent to reform the errors and abuses of society, but only that I would fain contribute my humble quota towards so good an aim; and if I can gain the public ear at all, I would rather whisper a few wholesome truths therein than much soft nonsense.

As to her identity, Anne insisted she was neither Currer nor Ellis and:

> In my own mind, I am satisfied that if a book is a good one, it is so whatever the sex of the author may be. All novels are, or should be, written for both men and women to read, and I am at a loss to conceive how a man should permit himself to

write anything that would be really disgraceful to a woman, or why a woman should be censured for writing anything that would be proper and becoming for a man.

Spoken like a true Brontë! However, since *Tenant* appeared to me as a stinging rebuke to *Wuthering Heights* (displaying the *real-world* consequence of cruelty), I was overcome with a desire to know Emily's thoughts.

One morning, I cornered her in the kitchen and asked just such a question.

"Honestly, I do not care." She hung the brass kettle over the stove.

"But Miss Anne is clearly attacking your work. And you two are so close! Surely you must feel something or other?"

She turned to me calmly. "Yes. I feel that Anne is overly religious in the conventional sense. She believes that Salvation is achieved only in Heaven. *I* have no interest in the celestial realm: to me, God is on earth, in us, everywhere. We shall always vary on this point, but in all other aspects, we are quite congenial."

I nodded. It took a truly great soul to soar above triviality and love the artist but not the art. All of the Brontës had this capacity, but I—raised in an artificial house—could not hope to achieve this generosity of spirit.

As it happened, two months after "the Bells'" return from London, every Brontë in Haworth took ill. The east winds—which Charlotte blamed for every malady—blew ferociously over the moors. Emily was most affected: she caught a cold from being outdoors and could not seem to recover. Each day, she appeared to us somewhat worse.

"Emily, is your health at all improved?" Charlotte would inquire.

No answer.

"Please—allow me to call the doctor."

"No poisoning medics."

She insisted on going to bed at ten, then coming downstairs at seven to perform her household chores. Her breathing was so harsh and labored that it gave me pain just to hear it.

On the fifteenth of December, she called me over to where she sat sewing. Her long fingers were so weak and her own form so emaciated that she dropped the work in her lap, unbeknownst to herself. I observed that her complexion was now paler than Anne's.

"I must impart—" Her coughing was truly brutal as she struggled to get out the words.

"Please—do not attempt to speak."

"I am ... I am ... the Nun." Despite her chronic condition, she managed a weak smile.

"*What?*" I refused to accept this confession, attributing it to her diminished state.

"Wanted—to scare you. Drive you off. I left the cellar door open knowing you would enter ... *I* was the one who took the yeast." Her whole body shook as her strangled lungs sought air.

I sought to imagine why. "You wanted to have all your spare time for writing?"

She nodded.

"Say no more, Miss Emily. I trust you feel differently now. Especially when I have given the world such a grand facsimile of Ellis!"

She smiled through her coughing.

"I do not wish to tire you. Let me leave you with this: your work—though not prolific—will live. *It* is immortal, even if we are not."

Since she was too weak to resist, I bent and kissed her on the forehead. "Good-bye, Emily," I said. I could not see through my tears.

Charlotte was beside herself. She took a long walk on the moors to gather a sprig of heather for her sister. When she returned and presented it, she saw that Emily was no longer able to recognize it.

On the morning of the eighteenth, Emily insisted on feeding the dogs, though she barely had strength to stand. Charlotte tried reading a soothing essay by Emerson but noticed that Emily did not follow.

The next day, Emily staggered downstairs as we all watched with horror. She refused aid even from Martha and struggled to comb her hair before the fire. The comb slipped from her hand and fell into the hearth, to be partially consumed by flame.

By noon, she was failing. She told Charlotte, "If you will send for a Doctor, I will see him now." Dr. Wheelhouse, the local physician, arrived, but it was far too late.

The entire family gathered as she lay on the dining room sofa. Mr. Brontë had no time to utter a prayer, for she died suddenly at two. She was thirty years old.

Charlotte became hysterical. Mr. Brontë continually begged her, "Charlotte, you must bear up. I shall sink if you fail me!" But her grief was so intense that she could not rise from the floor.

The funeral was three days later. This procession was a sad affair: at the head was Mr. Bell Nicholls, who conducted the service; Mr. Brontë and Emily's beloved Keeper; followed by Charlotte and Anne; myself; and Tabby and Martha.

Emily's stark wood coffin was narrow, for consumption had eaten her away. She was buried in the family vault of Saint Michael where her mother—and two long-gone (I assumed) sisters—lay. I noticed, numbly, that one had the given name of Maria, as had Mrs. Brontë.

I had never seen Charlotte so desolate. Her longing for M. Heger could not compare to this. She would later write to Ellen:

> I cannot forget Emily's death day. It becomes a more fixed, a darker, a more frequently recurring idea in my mind than ever. It was very terrible—she was torn conscious, panting, reluctant, though resolute, out of a happy life.

After the service, we all returned to the Parsonage. Keeper kept vigil at Emily's door, howling piteously for days. He voiced the feelings of us all.

Shortly after Emily's death, Charlotte opened her sister's writing desk to find five reviews comparing *Wuthering Heights* (unfavorably) to *Jane Eyre*. So she *did* care, after all, behind her stoic facade. Truly, she was the bravest person I have ever known. We shall never see her like again.

In the days after her passing, my preeminent thought was how to get word to Branwell. I had not recognized the mortality of Emily's state—not until the end. I had never expected her to die, for she seemed so much more than human. I would either have to journey back to Briarwood or send an emissary in my stead.

Then an event occurred that was so quick—so terrible —the decision was made *for* me. Anne took sick.

During the Christmas season, she seemed to contract the flu. Mr. Brontë called in a Dr. Teale from Leeds. Then came the dreaded diagnosis: she too suffered from tubercular consumption.

Like Emily, she had terrible pains in the side, and we could hear her deep coughs resound throughout the night. I inwardly debated what to do: send word to Branwell *now*, so he could share in the last days of his sister, or delay as long as possible so he might continue his work? Tortured, I consulted Charlotte to the degree that I was able.

"Do you think, Miss Brontë, that we should notify Mr. Branwell?"

"I sent a note regarding Emily, but never received a response. It is curious." She appeared terribly hurt. "I will write *again* about Anne. Perhaps not till mid-March. I do not wish to disturb the work that must shape his future career."

"Yes. That is sensible."

When the agreed-upon time arrived, I grabbed pen, paper, and ink.

16 March 1849
Haworth

Dear George,

Excuse me if I do not open with pleasantries, but I have a <u>desperate mission</u> to beg of you. Please say nothing to the family—especially <u>not</u> to Isabelle. There is a young man living in the hunting lodge at Briarwood—his name is Branwell Brontë. It is a very long story as to why he is there, which I do not have time to relate. There is only this to be told: his sister Emily died suddenly in December, and I fear his youngest sister, Anne, is also in grave danger.

Please, George—take the train to Worthing <u>with all conceivable haste</u> and deliver this to Mr.

Brontë. I know he would wish to be home during this desolate time.

Thank you, George—
<u>God Bless You</u>!
Your Fond Sister,
Maria

With trembling fingers, I handed the letter to Martha for delivery to the post. And waited. And waited. In the interim, I strove to assist Charlotte in her tender care of Anne.

Unlike Emily, Anne agreed to all of the "cures"—still with us today, alas!—for her malady: blisters applied to the side and teaspoons of cod liver oil. Rather than improve her health, these served only to nauseate her.

True to her character, Anne remained strong and serene. It was *Charlotte* who caused me anxiety, for I feared she would not survive the death of her last sister. All three of us would go out for a walk each day, though Anne's progress was more like a creep.

Still no word from Branwell! I wrote to George in April, pleading for some news. His reply arrived on the afternoon of Branwell's return to Haworth. My beloved swung through the Parsonage door, looking wan and stricken with care.

"Branwell!" Charlotte cried, throwing her arms about his neck and sobbing into his breast. How I envied her!

"Emily ..." he got out, then collapsed into tears as well. I wondered if the fragility of these two could withstand another blow.

"Anne!" He flung himself over her seated form, his face nestled against hers.

"It is good to see you. Please—do not come too close."

With reluctance, he rose to his feet. The doctor had counseled in January that Charlotte and Anne were no longer to share the same bed. We did not know in those days how quickly consumption spread: it remained until twenty years on to prove it a contagion.

The afternoon of Branwell's return, I walked out with him to the cemetery; past uneven, aboveground crypts.

"Do you wish to visit Emily's vault?"

"God no! There was a time when I relished morbidity, but no longer."

We leaned against a crooked gravestone.

"I hope you will forgive me for waiting so long to retrieve you. I thought of your work on the book."

"I am through volume two. But it no longer matters. *I* am the one who witnessed all of the deaths here: Maria, Elizabeth, Aunt, Weightman. Now there is Emily and dear Anne! It is all too much to bear."

He put his head in his hands and sobbed. Though the tears fell from my eyes, I sought to ameliorate his grief.

"Who *were* Maria and Elizabeth?"

"My two eldest sisters. They caught ill at Cowan Bridge—the 'Lowood' of *Jane Eyre*—then came home and died. Charlotte and Emily were away—it was *I* who saw them interred."

"I am very sorry." I put a soothing arm round his neck. "Who was Weightman?"

"A young clergyman—only twenty-eight—who died of a sudden of cholera. I was so fond of him—he was one of my dearest friends." He broke into renewed sobs.

Illumination flooded my brain. "Was he fair-haired? Handsome?"

"Yes, yes."

"My God! So Anne was in love with him! Have you seen her drawing or read her poems?"

Branwell lifted his head. "I did not make the association."

My desire was to chastise with a single word—"Men"—but he was in no condition to hear it. I sighed. "What is to be done now?"

"We watch Anne die, I suppose. It is all too, too much!"

I gave him a full-fledged kiss, but he seemed unaware. The Parsonage was seemingly cursed, for the cramped graveyard without had invisibly spread within.

The next month was shaded with grief, like Anne's drawing of Weightman. I could not ascertain how the Brontës remained standing. Yet—despite the high emotion of the remaining two eldest—it did: for a time.

In May, Branwell approached Anne, who sat quietly by the fire. "I have at last concluded my reading of *The Tenant*."

If possible, Anne went even paler.

"You have portrayed me as quite the insensitive brute! But unlike the vile Huntingdon, *I* have been redeemed."

"Yes, Brother." Anne spoke slowly as she fought for every breath. "Do not conflate yourself with Arthur. He is merely a warning to the world."

"All is forgiven," said Branwell, affectionately squeezing her hand. "And by the bye, Charlotte—" he turned to face her, causing her to wring her hands.

"*Jane Eyre* is *sui generis*; I see the Angrian roots, yet you have made of it so much more. *Brava*!" He solemnly knelt before her like a knight accepting the accolade.

"Thank you," Charlotte said simply. To her, the praise of her first collaborator was sweeter than any reviewer's.

As the month unfolded, Anne begged Charlotte to take her to Scarborough, where she had fond memories of holidays with the Robinsons. Charlotte staunchly refused, for she did not think Anne could be moved.

Finally, Dr. Teale proclaimed that sea air might do her good.

Anne's condition was grim: she was so weak and emaciated that she had to be lifted into the coach which Ellen kindly supplied.

Four of us were to embark—yet only three departed. Branwell was so overcome at the thought of another loss that he locked himself in his room, unable—or unwilling—to face us.

Outside on the Parsonage steps, Anne bade farewell to her father, Tabby, and Martha. She patted her spaniel, Flossy, on the head—all for the last time.

Charlotte, Anne, and myself boarded the one thirty train from Keighley to Leeds. Passengers displayed their kindness by helping Anne in and out of the coach. She desired to view anew the great cathedral of York Minster, which we did. She remarked, "If finite power can do this, what is the—" but, overcome with emotion, could not finish her thought.

At last we arrived at Scarborough, that normally gay seaside town. We took a room at Woods Lodgings, where Anne had stayed previously, but it was clear that, now, her visit would be but a short one.

Over the course of three days, Anne rode over the sand in a donkey-driven cart, chastising the boy driver for not treating the animal well. She even took the reins. She wished to attend church on Sunday, but this proved an impossibility. The next night, she watched a sunset from the lodge window, the glowing orb descending over an unruffled sea.

She wondered if she should return to Haworth, but the doctor who was summoned on the morrow did not recommend such a move.

28 May 1849. Anne rose at seven but was too weak to walk downstairs.

"Please. Let me assist you, Miss Anne."

Charlotte turned away—she could not bear to see her sister so. I gingerly picked Anne up—she seemed no heavier than a sparrow—walking carefully down the two flights. As my feet reached the first floor, the back of Anne's head fell against my own. *Oh my God*, I thought, *she is dead*!

I placed her on a chair, then sunk to my knees, sobbing. Amazingly, she extended her arms to succor *me*.

"It could not be helped, Maria. You did your best."

That was the very essence of Anne.

I hesitated, then blurted quickly, "You will be with Weightman now." She nodded and smiled.

Charlotte came down to join us. By and by, we lifted Anne and placed her on a sofa, where she prayed quietly.

"Are you any easier?" Charlotte asked.

"It is not you who can give me ease. But soon, all will be well through the merits of our Redeemer."

I had never seen such faith. The doctor appeared several times throughout that long afternoon. Like myself, he could barely fathom Anne's serenity.

Finally, at 2:00 p.m.—*the very same time as Emily*—Anne died. She was twenty-nine. Her last words were to her sister: "Take courage, Charlotte! Take courage." With a shaking hand, Charlotte closed Anne's eyes, then commenced weeping as if her whole body would break.

I did not think that one could bear such sorrow and still continue to exist. Yet Charlotte held up. She and I were the only mourners at the funeral, for Anne was buried in Scarborough. As we walked away from the newly dug mound, barren with no gravestone, Charlotte turned to me and issued an ultimatum.

GOOD-BYE

"You must quit Haworth," she said.

I looked down. I had been dreading this edict since the death of Emily.

"You know as well as I that the Parsonage is diseased. Two of its members have died; who knows how many more?"

"Why stay then?" I burst out. "Come and live at Harley Street—or Briarwood in the South! An army might be quartered in its vacant wings."

"I thank you for your kind offer. But my duty—more than ever—is to stay and look after Papa. Branwell and I are all he has remaining."

"What of Mr. Bell Nicholls? He *must* remain to assist Mr. Brontë in church. Would he not be a capable guardian?"

"Perhaps, but as a daughter, I am beholden to stay."

"I heard Mary say you were burying yourself in Haworth! There is no more reason for the Bells—Emily is gone! You could live in London and announce yourself: for once, bask in the fame which you deserve as no other."

Charlotte sighed. "Let us cease talking of me. Let us discuss *you*—and your imminent departure."

We walked past the Church of Saint Mary's in the midst of its renovation. The scaffolding and ropes seemed to hold the promise of something new.

"Under the present circumstance, our Establishment is closed. You have been with us five years now. High time to matriculate."

"I know it."

"Return to a happy life in a world beyond the graveyard."

Our journey to Haworth was solemn. The memories of Anne—and Emily—so recently gone!—haunted our coach with the vehemence of Cathy Earnshaw. It was a bitter homecoming.

Tabby and Martha saw to their chores in tears, while Flossy looked dejected at the absence of her kind mistress. Mr. Brontë, who had borne so much—the death of four children, his wife, sister-in-law, and best curate—withstood this last blow in silence. As with Anne, it must have been Faith that sustained him.

After a mournful tea, I began to look for Branwell. Mr. Brontë noticed my activity

"Still upstairs, I fear," he said to Charlotte and me. "And in a very bad way."

Charlotte's eyes flared with rage. "Selfish and weak as always! He will make himself a burden while we still shoulder the last!" She stormed into her father's study.

I cautiously mounted the stairs, pausing by Branwell's shut door. Not a breath sounded from within. With trepidation, I knocked softly, but my entreaty went unanswered, so I slowly pushed my way in.

I found him, nearly lost in a tangle of bedclothes, as dead to this unfeeling world as poor Anne and Emily. His head was in an unnatural position—neck high atop several pillows—and his eyes, though full open, revealed pupils the size of dots.

"Branwell, it is I—Maria."

Nothing. I raised my voice slightly.

"Branwell, I am come to report on Anne. Do you not wish to hear it?"

His unnatural gaze remained fixed. I assured myself that he lived, for I placed my ear to his chest. That heart—sensible to all beauty; and once overflowing with love—now beat but weakly.

I sat by him on the bed, taking his one hand into my two. "This cannot be the end," I told him. "You are *not* Arthur Huntingdon. You are a Brontë, a . . . a *Bell*, and you have wonderful writing in you. Remember—you are two-thirds complete on your novel!"

I looked at his face anxiously, but it was as if I were a specter greeting him in the Beyond. I saw then that my present cause was hopeless—that the succubus Opium lulled him again in her arms.

The next morning, I wrote a brief note to George detailing my London arrival. Afterwards, I approached a more onerous task: packing the detritus of five —*how they had flown!*—long years.

To accompany my original belongings, I now had a trunkful of books: those given by Smith; those supplied by the Brontës; and—how could I not?—the complete published works of the Bells. I lovingly packed Branwell's portrait and the first edition of my inscribed *Jane Eyre*.

Before going downstairs, I sat at my small table and penned a longer missive. I placed it, with unsteady hands, into Branwell's top dresser drawer. His physical attitude remained unchanged from yesterday. Though it required the will of Queen Victoria, I did not sob aloud as I bent to kiss his brow.

I found Charlotte in what was now her study, surrounded by a sprawl of notebooks: the extant manuscript of *Shirley*.

"I will take my leave," I told her, "though I would much rather remain. Are you certain you do not require a sister?"

"And *that* you shall always be! But I will not detain you in a house filled with white plague."

"Yet it is all right for *you* to stay?"

"That is my lot."

She rose, first offering me her hand, then hugging me round the waist. She was so miniscule that the top of her head stood a full half foot under mine!

"You must write—frequently," she told me, stepping back.

"And when you come to London, you must visit *me*."

"Agreed. We shall meet. Shortly."

"I count upon it. Do keep my informed as to how you get on with *Shirley*."

"It will be my most difficult enterprise. In light of —"

"Yes, but I know *you*. You *will* complete it, even in the face of Revolution! The other Bells would be so cross if you do not."

"I can hear Emily haranguing."

We both smiled, but our eyes were moist.

"Thank Heaven this is not a *final* good-bye!" I launched myself toward her.

"True. We still live."

"I cannot thank you—or your dear sisters—enough for what you have done. It has been . . . not only an honor, but a life-altering journey! I will always take utmost pride in having been the sole pupil at the Misses Brontë's Establishment."

We could no longer speak. I hugged Tabby and Martha, and even old Mr. Brontë. I gave Keeper and Flossy a pat, knowing that they were among the last living connections to Emily and Anne. I was glad when I heard the hired cart coming round the road. I do not think I could have stood there for one moment more.

VOLUME III

FIRST MEETING IN LONDON

As planned, I returned to London to take up my previous life. But I was a changed being. Everyone at home struggled to be kind: they knew of the Brontë's tragedies and treated me the same as a member of the grieving family.

Indeed, I could not walk two steps without recalling my loss: the utterance of German, reminding me of Emily, actually brought me to tears. In church, I thought wholly of Anne in her younger days: I could almost see her shy form as she averted her eyes from an eager Weightman.

With the buried intent to make myself suffer, I reread the younger Bells' novels. Such promise, such brilliance, extinguished prematurely as they were. I could not conceive how Charlotte endured with the loss of her dearest companions.

She wrote:

> Emily, Anne, are gone like dreams—gone as Maria and Elizabeth were twenty years ago. One by one I have watched them fall asleep on my arm and closed their glazed eyes. I have seen them buried one by one, and thus far, God has upheld me.

In all of my replies, I naturally asked about Branwell, receiving the same dismal response:

I fear that his "illness" has struck with its previous force and, if anything, has worsened. He staggers from the Bull to the druggist to home, in a state of near oblivion. Alas, there is now no Emily to retrieve him. Papa is deeply grieved.

This nearly drove me to madness. Here was the man I loved who had rendered himself insensible, yet I could not enter his home for fear of contagion. And once there, would might I do? He had rendered himself corpselike—even worse—for he dwelt in a sort of half life, like the mythic Fisher King. As with that personage, he had suffered a mortal wound, but where was the Grail Knight who could alleviate his pain?

It was the day after my return when George found me in the library: a vast, stained-glass affair that bore a resemblance to York Minster (though I was its sole inhabitant).

I sat immersed in *Wuthering Heights* on a high-backed chair, my feet barely touching the floor.

"Maria."

I started.

"I am so glad that you are at home! Now you may assist Athena as she prepares for our marriage."

"Will it be as grand as Queen Victoria's?"

"More so." He smiled. "Sister, there is something I must inquire of you—"

"I know. The 'red-haired gentleman.'"

"Yes."

"His identity I have revealed. *I* provided a refuge where he could compose his novel, for like all the Brontës, he writes. That is the whole of it."

"Indeed." George stared over at me on my oversized seat. From his thoughtful gaze, it seemed he too had gained some wisdom over the past years —at least, in matters of love.

"Brother, it is of little account," I said. "Mr. Branwell is distressingly ill and will likely follow his sisters. They are all extremely delicate." I wiped away my tears.

"I see." He stood for a silent moment. "I have said nothing of your note to me: not even to Athena, and certainly not to Father."

"For that I thank you most gratefully."

"Have a care, Maria. You are twenty-three, and Father rages daily regarding your unwed state. Mark my words: he will see you betrothed before the next decade arrives."

I lowered my head as he left. Never—not even in darkest Exile—had I felt so utterly alone.

My life's sole comfort lay in Charlotte's letters. She was a prolific correspondent, and often updated me as to her progress on *Shirley*. This novel was, of all things, a tale of the Luddite rebellion in Yorkshire. I thought it a curious choice—*for her*—but reserved judgment until publication.

This transpired in February 1849, a full eight months after I had vacated Haworth. Charlotte instructed Smith to send me the bound volumes, and eagerly, I devoured them. Alas, I found them to lacking. Written in the omniscient voice, the narrative did not include enough of *Charlotte herself*.

I discerned instantly that Shirley was modeled on Emily (had she wealth and position), but the love stories and action did not speak to my heart. Recalling Charlotte's struggles during the book's creation, I knew it was solely her will that kept her writing at all.

In November of that year, she at last visited London. As they had invited her, she stayed with Smith and his mother. This time, the family was fully apprised that Charlotte was Currer Bell.

My first glimpse of her in town was at a dinner thrown by Smith. His house at Westbourne Place was of course familiar to me from my last ignoble visit.

I disembarked from my carriage, noting the size of the house as compared to Harley Street: it could barely fill the servants' quarters! I managed to quell my snobbery as the Smiths came out to greet me: the women looking as if they had just encountered Lazarus!

"Good evening," I said to all. "I assume this proves—much to my misfortune--that *I* am not Ellis Bell. If you wish to hurl me into the street, I cannot for a moment blame you."

Of course not!" said Smith. "Incidentally, you gave a cracking performance."

"George!" his mother admonished.

"My actual name is Maria Shelby."

"Pleased to meet you—again!" Smith stuck out his hand.

I stepped into the drawing room to find a large party: solemn-suited men who looked like they breathed literature; and a tall, imposing figure I recognized from the frontispiece of his books.

He walked across the room, approaching a tiny woman clothed in deep black mourning. She looked terribly nervous and frightened. The man went over, bent down, and said quietly, "Shake hands."

Thus I was privileged to witness the first meeting of two Titans: Charlotte Brontë and William Thackeray.

We all went into dinner. It was arranged for Charlotte to sit at the bottom of the table, but she soon left her place and took a seat beside me.

"Ah Maria—how glad I am to see you! Those five men are the top critics of the day, and I confess I wish to bolt!"

I looked at the dark pentagon. Charlotte whispered that they were from the *Times, Athenaeum, Examiner, Spectator,* and *Atlas.*

As weighty a bunch that ever existed.

Smith did his hostly duty. "Gentlemen, this is Miss Brontë's great friend and pupil, Miss Shelby."

A deep chorus of "How'd you dos?" sounded, followed by silence. After an awkward silence of some duration, one of the critics spoke.

"Do you like London, Miss Brontë?"

Charlotte pondered for a moment. "Yes, and no."

Happily, my inward groans were inaudible. Charlotte seemed determined to disavow Currer Bell, but it was clear from the men's worship that they knew Jane Eyre's creator.

The *Times* reviewer made an attempt of his own. "I understand you saw the great Macready in *Othello* and *Macbeth.*"

"Yes. I found his performance both forced and artificial. It is my decided view that actors are suited to farce, yet when they attempt tragedy or Shakespeare, it is always an abject failure. As is the entire dramatic theatre."

This frank appraisal did not elicit a response. Smith put a hand to his head, while Thackeray slouched noticeably.

I decided to enliven Charlotte by broaching a favorite topic.

"Have you not stated, Miss Brontë, that real Art must contain, above all, Truth?"

She nodded. "*That* is my philosophy. Truth is better than Art; Burns's songs are better than Bulworth's epics." She glanced at her new tall friend. "Thackeray's rude, careless sketches are preferable to thousands of carefully finished paintings."

"That is the spirit!" Thackeray revived. There followed a lively discussion on everything from Dickens to Goldsmith. Charlotte, impassioned, put away her shyness and shone before the Eminent like the genius she was.

I exhaled, but after dessert, Smith made a joking faux pas that kindled the Brontë rage.

"Mr. Thackeray, may I interest you in a cigar?" He then quoted from *Jane Eyre*: "a subtle, well-known scent—that of a cigar—"

I groaned. He might as well have lit a match to *Charlotte*! Her demeanor as decorous Yorkshire Lady altered in a moment to fire-spewing wyrm. The heat rose on her cheeks, she clenched both her small fists, and resolutely refused to speak a single word more.

As Smith would later remark, no one could chill a dinner party quite like Charlotte Brontë.

The next morning, Charlotte arrived at 30 — — Harley Street on a solitary call. She looked around, amazed, obviously struck by the opulence. I did not introduce her to anyone after the "freeze" of last night.

I led her into the library, where I requested tea to be served. I motioned for her to sit; somehow, she managed to look like a queen in her outsized chair.

"This is quite the room," she remarked, her gaze taking in the curving expanse of books. "Does it house the immoral Shakespeare?"

"Yes, and Byron too!" We both smiled, then looked down sadly. "How do you fare, Miss Brontë?"

"Badly. Every night at nine, I walk an hour round the table, grieving for those who are gone. I fear I am trailed by ghosts."

I nodded, my eyes moistening.

"The evenings are the worst. During the day, I have my work, but by night, I find myself filled with rage."

"As do I." I paused. "Please, Miss Brontë, I beg you to allow me return and act as your companion. I am willing to risk *anything*." I must have sounded pathetic.

She reached over and clasped my hand. "I know your sentiments, Maria. But I cannot betray your father by removing you to the Parsonage. That would merely dignify me as a murderer."

We sat silent as the tea things were brought. I finally broached the matter uppermost in my mind.

"Mr. Branwell. Is he at all improved?"

"No. I fear he will be the next to descend to the family vault."

I burst into tears. "It is all so—unnecessary!" I cried. "Emily and Anne could not help it, but *he*—he is willfully seeking oblivion!"

As always at Branwell's mention, Charlotte's anger rose. "He has the emotions of a babe! He never learnt self-restraint, and was petted far too much as Papa's Golden Child."

"I fear he has turned into Huntingdon."

She nodded. "Anne was surprisingly prescient. Once I thought there was hope, but
now—"

"Is there *anything* one can do?"

"Pray. That is all that is left to him now."

We finished our tea in silence. When I next heard from Charlotte, it was on a mutually dear subject: her two departed sisters.

WEDDING THE FIRST

In the interval, there was to be a glorious wedding. After a lengthy engagement (prolonged by Athena's desire to dazzle London society), the date at last arrived: 22 June 1850.

She had drawn me into her planning, but this time I welcomed the distraction. The ceremony was to be held at Saint Andrew, Holborn (which witnessed the Norman conquest), followed by a large reception at home. There were to be so many chilled shrimp and crab legs, flowers, and fine wines, that it was entirely possible the Normans would reappear!

In a burst of sisterly fervor, Athena had assigned to me the position of bridesmaid, resulting in my requisite fitting for a ghastly dress. The service in the old church recalled a king's coronation, and I was somewhat shocked not to find the Queen in attendance.

At last, the vows were spoken, and the whole party repaired to Harley Street. The ballroom was done up so merrily, even *I* began to feel cheerful.

"Congratulations, dear Brother!" I threw my arms about George's neck. "At last. You have waited longer than Abraham for Isaac."

"That was but twenty-five years. I thank you, Sister. My sole wish is for *you* to be as blessed." Viewing his beaming expression, I was comforted by the knowledge that *he* at least married for love.

The elaborate reception seemed to stretch into the night: I had my fill of delicious seafood, then danced with George, Father—even Emma. At last it was Colin's turn.

"Miss Maria! It is *so good* to have you back. You do not seem the worse for wear."

"I am only a little older."

"Are not we all? On the subject of age, there is something I wish to ask you."

"Very well."

I was, in truth, not paying close attention—my gaze fell on the other dancers and an enormous multilayer cake.

"I myself am twenty-seven—high time to be finding a bride."

"Mmm hmmm."

"You know, I have always been fond of you, ever since George introduced us. I hope to make today an occasion of multiplied joy by requesting your hand in marriage."

A curtain of silence descended. I could not hear the private orchestra nor the laughter and discourse of guests—there was only the echo of my heart, thrice amplified in my ears.

"What did you say?" I asked, my senses returning in a rush.

"I just asked you to marry me! Maria—for I trust I may call you that now—are you quite well?"

I must have gone pale, for he escorted me to a chair on the periphery of the room.

"My dearest—" He bent over me.

"*No!* Please forgive me—I cannot accept your proposal."

His face flushed with embarrassment. "May I ask the reason?"

"It is nothing to do with you, Colin—*you* are perfectly fine. It is merely that . . . my heart belongs to another." I stared up at him ruefully.

"Ah. And where is this fortunate chap?" He glanced around as if to assault him.

"He is, unfortunately . . . ill, and cannot be present."

"Do I know the lucky gentleman?"

"No sir, you do not."

"I wish you all earthly happiness."

His tone belied his true feelings, more attuned to a speech by Emily: "The Devil take you then!"

Bowing coldly, he left me to myself. I saw him approach Alfred, lean forward, and impart something into his ear. Alfred's eyes widened, and he accosted Athena, lovely in her white bridal gown and surrounded by throngs of friends.

These whispers, I thought, *will grow loud and prove injurious.*

At last, as the moon saw them off, George and Athena entered their carriage, amidst many a shouted "Good luck!" and copious throwing of rice. Wishing to be quiet, I made my way to the back garden and sat on a wrought-iron chair. I was not there a half hour before Father sniffed me out, sweating in his formal attire.

"What is this intelligence abroad?" he cried.

I looked away forlornly, still in my fancy dress.

"Athena informed Mrs. P— —, who in turn informed *me* that you have entered into an engagement. *Without* my explicit permission."

"There is no engagement, Father."

"That merely worsens the matter! Who is this unknown gentleman to whom your heart is betrothed?" His breath was coming in huffs.

"You do not know him, Sir. At present, he is gravely ill and may not survive the month." I wiped away a stray tear.

"Well, that certainly assures me—not even *engaged* to a *stranger* on *his death bed*! What madness has taken hold of your senses?"

"Only that of love, Sir."

"'Love, love'! Do you think I loved your mother? She was heiress to a great fortune, and we united our two houses. *That* is the proper way for such things to be done."

"I must love the man I marry. I am sorry, Sir."

"From where does this fanciful notions derive? Those Brontës, with their illness and plagues and poverty? Would that I had never sent you to that accursed place!"

"I fear it is too late."

"Who is he?" Who is the scoundrel that dares court the daughter of a knight *without* asking said knight? Let him die with rapidity!"

"Please, Sir, it is no fault of his. Nor mine." I took a deep breath. " To quote Jane Eyre: 'I had not intended to love him; the reader knows I had wrought hard to extirpate from my soul the germs of love there detected; and now, at the first renewed view of him, they spontaneously arrived, green and strong!'"

"Silly women's novels! I *forbid* you to read them. And to visit this dying swain. You will, so to speak, 'extirpate him from your soul.' The only green germs I wish to see here will be sprouting from this lawn!"

I turned my head away.

"I merely ask you to do your duty—to marry a rich man. How difficult can such a task prove?"

He stormed back into the house as fast as his bulk would allow.

Reader, I was desolate. What more could I do? Emulate Helen Huntingdon and run away from it all? In which case I would be forced to work as a governess and suffer like Charlotte and Anne. I would be impoverished—

perhaps in a faraway land—with less hope than I had at present of seeing Branwell again.

The Brontës were wondrously clever, and they had taught me well, yet I could not think of a means to "extirpate" my pain. Of all my acquaintance, I knew but one person of genius: Charlotte. Would she accept my confidence? Or would her disgust with Branwell inspire her to thwart me? Of course, she was a *Brontë*, committed to the grave and beyond to the sanctity of Love. I weighed these disparate factors carefully over the forthcoming months.

RESURGAM

When Charlotte returned to Haworth, she set about compiling a book of her sisters' poems, along with *Agnes* and *Wuthering Heights*. She did not include *The Tenant*, for she thought it a mistake, which in my own opinion was itself one.

Still, she labored painfully over Anne's and Emily's work, and from her letters to me, I could tell she was deeply depressed. She wrote: "I fall into a condition of mind which turns entirely to the Past, to memory, and memory is both sad and relentless. This will never do."

Finally, an inexpensive version was put out by Newby in December 1850. Preceding the Bells' work was the now-famous "Biographical Notice of Ellis and Acton Bell."

To me, the final paragraphs were the most moving of all.

> What more shall I say about them? I cannot and need not say much more. In externals, they were two unobtrusive women; a perfectly secluded life gave them retiring manners and habits. In Emily's nature the extremes of vigour and simplicity seemed to meet. Under an unsophisticated culture, inartificial tastes, and an unpretending outside, lay a secret power and fire that might have informed the brain and kindled the veins of a

hero: but she had no worldly wisdom; her powers unadapted to the practical business of life; she would fail to defend her most manifest rights, to consult her most legitimate advantage. An interpreter ought always to have stood between her and the world. Her will was not very flexible, and it generally opposed her interest. Her temper was magnanimous, but warm and sudden; her spirit altogether unbending.

Anne's character was milder and more subdued; she wanted the power, the fire, the originality of her sister, but was well endowed with quiet virtues of her own. Long-suffering, self-denying, reflective, and intelligent, a constitutional reserve and taciturnity placed and kept her in the shade, and covered her mind, and especially her feelings, with a sort of nun-like veil, which was rarely lifted. Neither Emily nor Anne was learned; they had no thought of filling their pitchers at the well-spring of other minds; they always wrote from the impulse of nature, the dictates of intuition and from such stores of observation as their limited experience had enabled them to amass. I may sum up all by saying, that for strangers they were nothing; but for those who had known them all their lives in the intimacy of close relationship, they were genuinely good and truly great.

This notice has been written, because I felt it a sacred duty to wipe the dust off their gravestones, and leave their dear names free from soil.

CURRER BELL

I could not have been gladder that the shroud of anonymity had been lifted from Ellis and Acton. Still, I took issue with Charlotte's assessment: her sisters *were* in fact learned; Emily hardly required an interpreter, and Anne, though quiet, assuredly was not "nun-like." Charlotte seemed to reflect more on *herself* than her sisters: she did not like it when Emily disagreed; and undoubtedly felt hurt that Anne did not confide in her. However, on these points I did not quibble. Charlotte spoke lovingly of those she had loved and the loss was so much more hers than mine or anyone else's.

I had seen her again in London, in June. She looked older and tired, but this was to be expected in light of her many burdens.

During this last visit, I was privileged to be present at two sublime events (though the second counts for double, so one might say there were three).

Charlotte stayed with the Smiths, this time, in their new house at Hyde Park Gardens. One morning, I stopped by to call and witnessed what may be deemed a true clash of the Titans.

Charlotte—all four feet ten of her—was in the process of scolding Thackeray, (who was at least six feet tall), in the vestibule. It must have been a lengthy screed, for Thackeray looked enervated. This is where I entered.

"Sir, you do not treat your vows as Artist with the seriousness it merits! It is fine to mock fools in books, but *you* are a man with a mission, and I fail to see why you continually make light of it."

"Really, Miss Brontë—" Thackeray managed to get out.

"You devote most of your time to young women, each a perfect Blanche Ingram! What care you what they wear to a ball, or what hat they parade at the opera? *You* should be occupied strictly with fashioning books—*not* with Fashion."

Thackeray hung his head. It was really quite a sight: this tiny woman, filled with near-religious fever, hectoring the Great Man on his art! I wanted to laugh but could not, and instead decided to divert Charlotte.

"Pardon me, Miss Brontë, did you not wish to show me the Turners at the Gallery? I know you admire them so."

Thackeray turned with gratitude. Perspiration dripped from his forehead as he grabbed his hat and rushed out, not unlike a chastised schoolboy.

"Good Heavens, Miss Brontë. What was the length of that lecture?"

"I believe a good two hours. I only hope he is the better for it."

I—who knew London society—gave an inward chuckle. The earnestness of a Charlotte could only be found in church, where it was generally more dumb show than Belief. This woman poured her whole soul into her art and could not understand why others would not follow. In my decided view, *hers* was the correct course.

Thackeray might have thought otherwise. He informed Mrs. Gaskell later that he actually *feared* Miss Brontë!

The second event of note occurred at a luncheon hosted by Smith. Present was G.H. Lewes, the critic who had praised Charlotte when she first burst onto the scene. I saw he was in his thirties, possessed of a large forehead offset by ferocious whiskers.

Over the light repast, Lewes thought to make a joke. He leaned over the table to Charlotte. "There ought to be a bond of sympathy between us, Miss Brontë, for we have both written naughty books."

I steeled myself, waiting for the lava to flow.

"I do not know what you mean!" Charlotte cried. She shot up from her chair, storming out a side door.

Smith made vague motions to stand.

"You may stay where you are, Mr. Smith," I said. "Let me go to calm her."

"Thank you," Smith said weakly. I could see that Lewes's hands were shaking.

I exited the same door as Charlotte, surprised to find her engaged in discourse. She spoke with a youngish woman who had been alone in the garden. Forgive my frankness, Reader, but the stranger made Charlotte look handsome. She had a very simple hairstyle, prominent nose, and large, piercing light eyes.

I stood awkwardly for a moment.

"Miss Maria Shelby," Charlotte said, and I could tell that she had quietened, "this is Miss Mary Ann Evans."

"How do you do?" I asked.

"Very well, I thank you."

A question must have been written across Charlotte's brow and my own: *why* was Miss Evans banished as if she had the plague?

"I perceive your curiosity. I am not permitted in the Smiths' for they have daughters within. I am, as they say, 'not received.'"

"Whatever was your crime?" cried Charlotte. She was one who could not tolerate injustice.

"It is rather a long saga, but allow me to abridge it for you. Mr. Lewes is still married, though his wife has borne four children out of wedlock. Since he is legally listed as 'the father,' he is unable to divorce her. Which forces me, I fear, into a kind of concubinage."

Charlotte—as daring an author who ever lived—retreated behind a mask of decorum.

"But you seem so intelligent and nice!"

Miss Evans smiled. "'Conventionality is not morality.'"

Charlotte looked surprised. "You know me then."

"I do. And may I say, Miss Brontë, you are not only a supreme genius but an inspiration."

Charlotte was taken aback.

"Indeed, I hope to model myself on *you* one day."

Smith tentatively entered the garden, and seeing our infamous companion, sought to shoo us away like chickens. Charlotte and I both bowed to Miss Evans. I would not find out for nearly a decade—when she began publishing her own books—that Mary Ann Evans had a nom de plume: Mr. George Eliot. And *I* had been present at her meeting with Currer Bell!

As we stepped back into the house, Charlotte took up her friend's cause.

"George, why is it that Miss Evans must suffer pariahdom, while Mr. Lewes—just as culpable in her shame—is admitted without impediment?"

The two gentlemen hemmed and hawed. I almost smiled when I viewed their discomfort, but then I remembered Miss Evans—seemingly the brainiest of the three—exiled to the garden.

The remainder of the luncheon went well, though I—and I know Charlotte—frequently thought of the Exile. I peered into the tiny side garden, but she was nowhere to be seen. I hoped that she had the means to make her way home.

One detail of that day stood out to me like a bas-relief: it was Charlotte's familiarity toward Smith. Now he was "George"; now she would take his suggestion to sit for a portrait by Richmond; and he proposed that the two of them (accompanied by his sister of course) travel together to Scotland. I berated myself for not having discerned this previously. Reader, my power of observation was clearly in decline.

As we rose to depart, Charlotte shook hands with Lewes and asked him, "We are friends now, are we not?"

Lewes seemed puzzled. "Were we not always then?"

"No—not always."

It appeared that the critic had forgotten his review of *Shirley*, written during domestic travails. It began: "The grand function of woman is, and ever must be, maternity."

He went on to note that the book was "the very antipathy to ladylike" and that "women were only half-educated." No wonder the great women authors all cloaked themselves in pseudonyms!

To my utter amazement, Charlotte later decided to make the trip with Smith! She met up with him in Edinburgh, then toured all the grounds frequented by Walter Scott.

She wrote to me: "My six or eight years of seniority, to say nothing of lack of all pretention to beauty and c., are a perfect safeguard. I should not in the least fear to go with him to China." I thought perhaps she protested too much . . .

Yet when Charlotte returned to Haworth, her loneliness almost felled her. She wrote to me in London:

> I cannot describe what a time of it I had after my return from London, Scotland &c. There was a reaction that sunk me to the earth. The deadly silence, desolation, solitude were awful. The craving for companionship, the hopelessness of relief were what I should dread to feel again.

I wanted to flee to Haworth, but what could I as a prisoner do? Father harangued me every hour to choose some son of fortune, and persisted in hosting endless trumped-up balls. It appeared that Isabelle was about to secure Lord Kirby, which sent Father into apoplectic fits.

Then, as Charlotte proceeded to write her fourth novel, *Villette*, I received a letter from her that filled me with exquisite anguish: Branwell, it seemed, no longer frequented his room — had gone missing while Charlotte was away, whereabouts unknown!

This seemed the final blow. To where could he have removed himself? He had not been spied in his usual haunts: the Black Bull, the druggist, Bradford. I even begged Charlotte to search the Parsonage graveyard, for I feared the worst. So many images crowded my mind: Had he *really* absconded to Paris, to take up the career of painter? Or was he in Scarborough, visiting dear Anne's grave? All I knew was that he had communicated nothing.

At night, without fail, I buried my face in my pillows and sobbed like one deranged. My days were no more vibrant Charlotte's description of hers. I merely mimed the motions of eating and did not respond when called. In truth, I became another Ellis without benefit of artifice.

My pain actually deepened when Charlotte sent to me the first volume of *Villette*.

In 1851, I read:

> My heart almost died within me; miserable longings strained its chords. How long were the September days! How silent, how lifeless! How vast and void seemed the desolate premises! How gloomy the forsaken garden — grey now with the dust of a town summer departed. Looking forward at the commencement of those eight weeks, I hardly knew how I was to live to the end. My spirits had long been gradually sinking; now that the prop of employment was withdrawn, they

went down fast. Even to look forward was not to hope: the dumb future spoke no comfort, offered no promise, gave no inducement to bear present evil in reliance on future good. A sorrowful indifference to existence often pressed on me—a despairing resignation to reach betimes the end of all things earthly.

Villette left me in confusion, being two things at once: it was a bittersweet look at Charlotte's days in Brussels, with Monsieur appearing this time as "M. Paul Emanuel," the "dark little man" with the nature of a "black and sallow tiger." It also depicted her infatuation with Smith: he was the handsome "Dr. John" who assuages Lucy Snow's loneliness and might be more than a friend.

I put my head in my hands. I knew—as instinctually as Charlotte should have—that Smith would never marry her, nor would his mother permit it. That fine matron would not see the holder of her hopes united with an older, plain woman who wrote "coarse" novels and hailed from the uncouth North. How could Charlotte, with all her brains, not see what was so overt to me?

She returned to London that year to view The Great Exhibition, held at the Crystal Palace (in fact, she would go fully *five times*). She was also in attendance at several lectures by Thackeray. He mortified her when he presented her thus: "Mother, you must allow me to introduce you to Jane Eyre!" Half the room heard, and when Thackeray finished his lecture, he bounded down the stairs to solicit Charlotte's opinion. All of this unsought attention led to a second tirade from Charlotte: in private, thankfully, and one I did not witness. Mr. Smith has been kind enough to inform me of this event.

I finally caught up with my friend when Sir David Brewster (inventor of the kaleidoscope) toured us round the Exhibition. I could discern that after two hours, Charlotte had had enough of Science, so she and I escaped. Somehow, we found ourselves at the side of a garishly costumed "elephant."

"What do you make this?" I asked her. In truth, the Palace was dazzling, with its convex clear glass ceiling, marble sculptures, and huge spurting fountain.

"It is an excessively bustling place. But in my view, its wonders appeal exclusively to the eye and rarely touch the heart or head."

I laughed. If that was not pure Charlotte than I knew not what was! I noticed that she looked rather hurt.

"I am sorry, Charlotte. I was not laughing at *you*, but at your characteristic frankness." (We had become close enough now for me to drop all formality.)

She smiled.

"How *are* you, generally? Your letters of late are alarming. You spirits seem terribly low."

"I am fair," she said, though I disbelieved her. "I have my work and that is something."

"Yes, I should say *Villette* is so far your absolute best."

She beamed. "Thank you."

I had a covert agenda and tried to make a mask of my face. "How goes your visit with the Smiths?"

"Well . . . George—Mr. Smith—is exceedingly pressed at the office. Oftentimes, he will not return until three in the morning! I fear all is not well with the firm, but I dare not inquire."

I nodded. I knew, from George's gossip, that Smith's partner in India had embezzled a goodly sum. Still, I did not wish to trouble my already troubled friend.

"And your health?"

"I am fine. *I suffer from no particular ailment.*" She made this pronouncement loudly.

I wondered: *does someone spread rumors about that she is touched with consumption?*

I next broached the question of most concern to me. "And Branwell? Any news?"

"None. He has vanished, perhaps forever, like Emily and Anne, Maria and Elizabeth."

"You do not believe . . . ?" My question hung in the air, rising toward the pachyderm's finery.

"I do not know," she answered, her eyes overfilling with tears. "Why can he not send a letter? Yet more Byronic behavior! Perhaps he has returned to that Robinson Medusa."

We both look surprised at this utterance.

"I did not mean that."

"No."

The two of us half ran in our long skirts to catch back up to Sir David. I saw nothing further in the Palace; I merely searched the crowd for any sight of Branwell.

"VILLETTE, VILLETTE—HAVE YOU READ IT?"

It was winter, 1852. Father had set down a mandate: either I choose an eligible suitor, or he would do it *for* me. My consent no longer mattered. By this time, George and Athena had produced my nephew, Martin. He was exceedingly precious, and since his parents resided at 20—— Harley Street, I spent much of my time rocking the baby and playing with him.

I had not heard a word from Branwell—nor, to my knowledge, had anyone—that entire long year. Inwardly, I debated: should I give him up for dead; find another and put Father at his ease? Perhaps have a Martin of my own . . . ?

Yet each time I closed my eyes, I saw Branwell's wild red hair; felt his tremendous life force; the phantom touch of his lips on mine. No! I would not betray him, even if it cost me my happiness. *I* would not seek matrimony with one I could not love—nor certainly one I despised. For many a month that year, I dwelt on Helen Huntingdon: her calm inner strength and outward daring. When I thought of her, I saw the face of Anne.

At last, Charlotte completed her masterpiece *Villette*. To my—and many readers'—amazement, Lucy falls in love with M. Paul, her beloved Master in Brussels. This, more than anything, showed me that Charlotte's heart had turned: she had been rebuffed by Smith and returned (literarily) to her old love.

I confess I was glad. Charlotte was a woman formed much like myself: we could *truly* love but once, yet that love was strong as Cathy's for Heathcliff; Jane's for Mr. Rochester. There was nothing casual in the nature of our attachment. As M. Paul says to Lucy: "What do you start for? Because I said passion? Well, I say it again. There is such a word, and there is such a thing."
No two women alive knew this more than Charlotte and me.

Villette was an absolute triumph. I was told in later years that Mary Ann Evans had written:

> I am only just returned to a sense of the real world about me, for I have been reading *Villette*, a still more wonderful book than *Jane Eyre*. There is something almost preternatural in its power.

One month later she would write: "*Villette. Villette—* Have you read it?"

Lewes redeemed himself—professionally—with "Every page, every paragraph, is sharp with individuality. It is Currer Bell speaking to you."

Of course, there were the usual naysayers. Matthew Arnold decried the book as filled with "hunger, rebellion, and rage." Apparently, he disliked *Villette* after having met Charlotte: she did not meet his standard of typical feminine beauty.

More surprisingly, Charlotte's writer friend, Harriet Martineau, felt that in her work, Miss Brontë was obsessed by Love. Charlotte answered her back:

> I know what love is, as I understand it, and if man or woman should be ashamed of feeling such love,

then is there nothing right, noble, faithful, truthful, unselfish in this earth as I comprehend rectitude, nobleness, fidelity, truth, and disinterestedness.

There were the usual cries of "unladylike," with Ann Mozley leading the charge: accusing Charlotte of being "alien from society and amenable to none of its laws." I noted that she now dismissed these words with a sneer. Her manifold tragedies—the recent deaths of two sisters, the probable one of a brother, the deflation of all her romantic hopes—had forged her into a being nearly the equal of Emily.

When she wrote to protest Mozley, informing her that she was "alien from society" since she lived in a remote village and was (in all likelihood) the last survivor of six, *The Christian Remembrancer* apologized. I was so proud of Charlotte; she had blasted her critics and made them bow down before her!

Shortly after *Villette*, I experienced an upset that truly put me in danger and nearly satisfied Father's wishes.

I was sitting at home as was my custom, reading more of *The Three Musketeers*. Our butler Wood entered the sitting room, preceding a tall thin figure I had met on several occasions: Lord Nigel himself. I rose, curtsied, and beckoned for him to sit. I remained silent, waiting for him to announce the purpose of this visit.

"Miss Maria Shelby," he began.

"Yes, Lord Nigel." As always, I had forgotten his surname!

"I have noticed you."

I inclined my head, wondering where this was tending.

"You are the special friend of Miss Isabelle, are you not?"

This was easy enough to agree to. "I like to believe so."

"She is rather annoying, would you not concur?"

How unspeakably rude. Immediately, I stiffened. "If I *am* her special friend, then surely I do *not*." I fought the desire to rise from my seat and depart.

He crossed his lanky legs, showing off his hand-tooled boots.

"In any case, I prefer yourself to her. I like fair women—I have a weakness for flaxen hair. And it is apparent that our union would be advantageous. . . to the mutual purse."

I felt as if he proposed that we start a business.

"And where shall the firm be located? Cornhill Row?"

He did not take my meaning. He removed a cigar from his breast pocket.

I stood. "Sir, I find the whole of this discourse distasteful. I *beg you* never to approach me again. I might suggest you uphold your gentleman's honor and propose to Miss Isabelle, who rightfully expects the event."

"Ha! Full of fire, eh? I like that! I shall take the matter direct to Sir Shelby."

He rose from his chair, and we faced each other like duelists.

"I leave you, Sir, with the utmost of contempt. I pray there is no repetition of this offer." I turned coldly and departed the room.

Still, I was shaking. All of London had been present as he romanced my friend. Would Father grant his permission to such a public cad? I could only hope that his prizing of Appearance would incline him toward the negative.

That night was not a good one, for I wrestled with indecision. Even if Father demurred, was it my *duty* to inform Isabelle? Let her know the manner of man she planned to spend the rest of her life with? Or would this merely dash her hopes, leading to a misery that might well last forever? This was a moral dilemma to which I was not an equal. Where oh where was Emily when I most required her?

The next day brought an unexpected call. As Wood entered the dining room, where I still sat at breakfast, I felt an assault of dread. Had my "suitor" reappeared to put forth his case to Father?

I looked down, focusing on my poached eggs. I absolutely refused to meet the eye of my oppressor.

"Mr. Brontë," Wood drawled.

I raised my head cautiously. I expected to see Mr. Brontë, a prisoner of his cravat. No doubt he had rushed to London, the bearer of some grim tidings.

Instead, my gaze met a red-haired gentleman! Ignoring Wood and the other footmen, I threw myself into his arms.

"Branwell! Where have you been? I feared that you were lost!"

His response was delayed by a series of deep kisses.

"My love, I am sorry to have troubled you. I returned to Briarwood after I stumbled—literally—upon your note."

He removed a single creased sheet from his vest. I recognized my own hand from the letter that I had left in his dresser. He now held it up.

Dearest Branwell:

I have no choice but to depart—Charlotte will not permit me to stay. Remember: <u>You</u> are no Arthur Huntingdon—<u>you are a Brontë</u> and artist of great power.

<u>I believe in the power of your creation</u>—do not cease until you have realized it!

> <u>All</u> of your sisters and I eagerly await your next work.
> I love you,
> MS

"It was this that returned me to life! But I wished to reappear with the physical proof of my efforts."

He placed a weighty ream of paper on the table. "*And the Weary Are at Rest*. Fair copy. I am en route to deliver it to Newby!"

I felt as if I remained still and the room itself spun about me. "Has he agreed to its publication?"

"Indeed! He deems it a worthy successor to *Wuthering Heights*."

"No higher praise in this world."

Branwell sighed, and I knew he thought of Emily. "Nor any other."

One heavy concern tugged at me. "He does not believe this is a work by Ellis?"

"Oh no—I am *Bertram* Bell, and he has witnessed me in the flesh."

We held each other close, and I breathed in his essence. Not of cigar smoke and mastery, but light cologne and partnership. These moments seemed to last longer than my full five years at the Parsonage.

Of a sudden, we both spoke at once:

"I have something to tell you."/"There is something I must impart."

We both laughed.

"What is *your* news?" I asked him.

"Not good, by any means." He sat down at the table and eyed the endless silver trays. "May I?"

"Of course."

He seized an empty plate, piling it high with eggs and meat.

"I am afraid . . . that I saw Ellen's brother, Henry, at the station and he imparted something incredible. There appears to be a good chance that Charlotte will accept Old Whiskers. By whom I mean, Arthur Bell Nicholls."

"*No*," I cried, "this is a false report! Her heart has returned to her first love—have you not read *Villette*?"

"I have, and recognize its genius. Yet whatever she truly feels, she is turning to Father's old curate. Alas, he has declared himself."

I groaned in a most unladylike fashion. "Bell Nicholls is stiff as a board—he is a Puseyite! The Highest of the High Church."

"Yes."

"Who is it that he wishes to marry? His rector's pious daughter, or the novelist Currer Bell?"

"The former, to be sure."

"What appeal can be possibly hold for Charlotte?"

Branwell motioned for a dark-clothed footman to pour him some tea. "He is a man. He is in Haworth. He is her only prospect."

"G——d—— that George Smith!" I yelled.

"'Dr. John?'"

"The same." I paced the length of the table—which was some distance—and with a wave dismissed the servants. "Has she accepted?"

"No. She thinks it will kill Papa."

"That is the *one* positive to be gleaned from his cruel selfishness."

"Yes."

I stopped by Branwell's chair and sat down beside him, as he took my hand in his. "You understand who M. Paul really is—who *Rochester* is?"

He looked up at the ceiling and chuckled. "Do you take me for a simpleton? Of *course* it is M. Heger!"

"That letter—at the Red House. Charlotte confessed her feelings for him to Mary."

"And described it at length in two books. I hardly think it a secret."

"That still leaves the primary question, whose answer I have sought for years!"

Branwell arched an eyebrow. I grabbed him by the shoulders.

"Does Monsieur love her as she loves him?"

He removed me from his person. "I doubt it. He is a married man: to him, she is just another worshipful schoolgirl—one with great talent, to be sure."

"And would this not attract him? As a *Professor of Literature?* Do they not share a complete affinity of taste?"

"That is my understanding. But love is not purely of the mind—there must be a physical attraction." He winked over at me.

"Yes, but we know from Charlotte's books he is hardly a handsome man. No Smith in the fresh bloom of youth."

"Agreed. But men in general require beauty, and that, I fear, evaded my sisters, save for the lovely Anne."

I stood, defiant. I yelled as I never had: *"And who is this man to demand a Blanche Ingram when he has in his reach Jane Eyre?"*

Branwell's eyes widened. "Well, he *is* a man."

"But a *shallow* one? He is a being who worships Intellect, and it is my belief—I feel it like a premonition!--that he reciprocates Charlotte's love."

"Have you any proof? He refused to answer her letters."

"Perhaps Madame forced his hand."

"Speaking of whom—"

"I know. It is wrong to encourage such love. You of all people comprehend. Yet I find myself under a strange compulsion: I *must* discover if the master shares his pupil's passion!"

Branwell sighed. "*That* is a weighty mission. If you put such words in writing, be assured he will never respond. And what of Madame? As stealthy a spy as ever lived, per Charlotte. If *she* gains hold of the letter, you have tried and sentenced Monsieur, while he may be wholly guiltless." He spread his hands in a gesture of helplessness.

"I am not going to write."

We locked gazes. Branwell, by virtue of being a Brontë, knew exactly my meaning.

"Even *I* find this lunatic!" he cried. "And I am a well-known lunatic."

"Mad or not, I shall attempt it. We must put a halt to Bell Nicholls' suit!"

A Journey to a Foreign Land

Though Branwell disdained my scheme, his love for me was strong, and he agreed to act as accomplice. That evening, he appeared in the back garden of 30—— Harley Street at precisely 4:00 a.m. I crept through the sleeping house, wielding a small (for me) case that contained my remaining money and a few changes of clothes.

We snuck down the vacant streets, taking an errant cab straight to London Bridge Wharf. We both searched for the Ostend packet, finally finding it docked and silent.

"Hey there!" Branwell hailed a returning seaman lurching portside from drink. "Can you row us out to your ship?" He flashed a five-pound note.

"Course—aahhht for ya and the lydy."

Branwell handed us into a dingy, then seized its oars as we slid over the water. At last, with his assistance, we were all safely on board.

As dawn was long upon us, the captain could be spotted on deck.

"Wot ya want?" he yelled.

"Passage to Ostend," I answered. I flashed a fistful of notes. "At the double, if you please."

The rough captain became a different man. He gave a mock bow. "Coytanlee, me lydy. We'll 'rrive in four'een'ours."

"Thank you."

He seized the notes. "Oh nah—thank *ya*."

Branwell and I stood at the rail for the passage's duration. I enjoyed the cold ocean spray on my face, and he the rolling waves at the northernmost tip of the channel. I knew that the sea held a special attraction for the Brontës: when Charlotte viewed it for the first time, she told me she actually wept.

It was December and very crisp. I was glad to be wrapped in my warmest coat and gloves. Branwell's attire was lighter, but he was used to Arctic climes. As he held me for the entirety of the journey, I felt warm in his embrace. Whatever awaited us back in London—or ahead, in Belgium—seemed an ocean's-length away.

At last, we arrived landside. We took the railway to Brussels (unlike Charlotte in the early forties, when she had to rely on the diligence). It was now nighttime and very dark: I could not report if Charlotte's portrayal of Belgium—"bare, flat, and treeless"—was accurate or not. Had it even been light, we were both so fatigued that we slept the entire train journey.

Finally, a porter awakened us. "Brussels!" he pronounced in a heavy French accent.

We nodded, disembarking at last.

"This foreign travel is tiring," said Branwell. "No wonder Charlotte is always so cross."

I elbowed him. "We must get to the Pensionnat Heger!"

"It is near midnight: somehow, I do not think the Hegers will be overjoyed to greet us."

I nodded. "Where may we go to spend the night?"

"Charlotte said that when she first arrived, she stayed at l'Hotel d'Hollande, by the diligence terminal."

"Good. Let us find it."

We walked wearily toward the old terminal, then into the hotel, where Branwell secured a room. I, not wishing to lie (for once!) about our marital status, half covered my face with my shawl.

"*Votre nouvelle mariée est très timide, je vois!*"[11]

"*Oui.*"

The thin innkeeper leaned over his counter. "*C'est la meilleure façon de les recevoir—pas d'ennuis!*"[12]

Branwell laughed. "*Oui, monsieur—je suis tout à fait d'accord.*"[13]

After the landlord showed us upstairs, I hit my companion on the arm. "Surely you do not believe that?"

"No, no! I am merely trying to ease the locals."

"The French," I grumbled. "They treat women worse than the English."

"Yet you desire my sister to marry one."

"Monsieur is *not* French—he is Belgian!"

"Pfftt! Fine difference."

Branwell collapsed on the overstuffed bed—the only one in the room. He removed his coat and vest.

"I desire to sleep for the next three days. My love, do not awaken me over-early. Or should I say, '*Ma fiancée.*'"

"I do not recall being *formally* asked—only by two other gentlemen whom I did not like."

He bolted upright. "*That many*, already? Then I must set things aright!" He bent down on one knee and placed his head against the folds of my dress.

"Maria Shelby—daughter of kings, daughter indeed of the mighty sea god Poseidon—"

I laughed.

"—saved from a life of ignorance by my good sisters. Saved from two loveless marriages by my own good self. I beg you, in the name of God and his holies—Cowper,

---

[11] "Your new bride is very shy, I see!"

[12] "That is the best way to receive them, no trouble!"

[13] "I couldn't agree more!"

Bryon, and Shakespeare—I humbly ask you to be my wife!"

This was one proposal I was glad enough to receive. I lifted him up and said, "Yes. I accept." With those words, I threw off the yoke of servitude required by home, Father, and "Duty."

"May I kiss the bride?"

I pushed him away. "No. Now that we are betrothed, there shall be no more kisses until Mr. Bell Nicholls pronounces us man and wife."

"What have I done?" Branwell cried, but he smiled. He motioned me toward him and we both reclined, exhausted, upon that feathery bed. We slept in each other's arms until the late morning, which dawned cold and fair.

"We must go!" I jolted awake and nudged him. We both prepared our toilettes, so as not to frighten Monsieur with a savage English front.

On our way out we passed the innkeeper, who gave Branwell a playful wink. At last, we stood before our destination, one we only knew from a book: 32 Rue d'Isabelle. The Pensionnat Heger.

M. PAUL EMANUEL

It was *exactly* as Charlotte described: the school was in a small cobbled street sunk below the Park Royale. High, worn steps led to a door bearing the nameplate "Pensionnat de Demoiselles" with a name inscribed below: "Monsieur Heger."

"That is odd," I told Branwell. "*Where* is Madame's name? It was present in *Villette*."

He shook his head and knocked. A woman with a small white cap opened the door a crack and cautiously peeked out.

"*Bonjour*," I greeted her. "*Nous sommes des amis de Monsieur Heger.*"

She did not move an inch. "*Qu'est-ce que vous désirez?*"[14] she asked with suspicion.

"*Nous sommes des professeurs,*"[15] I lied shamelessly. "Fluent in both English and *Français*."

She seemed unconvinced.

"*Nous sommes les amis de Charlotte Brontë,*"[16] I said.

Her expression changed noticeably to something between horror and shock.

"May we come in?" I asked in French.

She thought for a moment, then ushered us into a cold salon and backed out through the unfolded door.

---

[14] "What is your business?"

[15] "We are teachers."

[16] "We are friends of Charlotte Brontë"

Branwell and I sat there as a full hour ticked away. It could not have been made more clear: Monsieur was not in a hurry to meet any friend of Charlotte's.

At last, we heard a welcome sound: the joyous chatter of children. A small man dressed all in black burst in, followed by *six* of his progeny, ranging in age I should say from sixteen to seven.

Even without his brood, there was no mistaking M. Constantin Heger. In every aspect and feature, he was M. Paul Emanuel: the selfsame cropped black hair, wide forehead, and irritability. The only element lacking was his usually present cigar.

"Monsieur," I said, rising (our following discourse was conducted entirely in French). "I am Miss Maria Shelby from London and this is Charlotte and Emily's brother, Mr. Branwell."

Heger's dark eyes widened. The *bonne* must not have delivered our message, for he was taken unawares.

"Children, children go!" he shouted in imperious tones. *This* was assuredly one Master accustomed to being obeyed.

The three of us now stood facing one another. Monsieur was so agitated that he failed to ask us to sit.

"Miss Charlotte—she is well?" he queried at last. I could not say if his voice quavered or if that was its natural state.

"Yes," Branwell answered, "but my sisters Emily and Anne have passed."

"Miss Emily!" Monsieur cried. "What an extraordinary mind! I am devastated by this loss." He looked it.

"She wrote a novel," I said.

"I am hardly surprised."

"Have you read it?"

"No. I fear there are no translations in French."

"Charlotte is an author as well. One of the most celebrated in England!"

His expression reflected both pride—at having taught her—and something tinged with regret.

I pressed on. "I trust that Monsieur and family are well?"

"The children, yes. They are all in exemplary health. Though I am sorry to relay that my second wife, Mme. Heger, died of a low fever last year."

"*Second* wife?" both Branwell and I exclaimed.

"Yes. My first wife and daughter died of cholera. The loss still affects me deeply."

"Justine Marie!" I cried.

"Marie-Josephine, in fact." He looked puzzled and surprised. "How did you know?"

"I read the book. *Villette*."

"I take it that is Miss Charlotte's?"

"*One* of them. Yes."

He started to move excitedly, as if animated by a force outside himself. "Come. Let me show you something."

He led us through two large doors revealing three spacious schoolrooms. He strode into one, the *estrade* where the teacher's desk rested at the ready for its occupant.

"See?" He walked toward the middle of the room, reverently lifting the lid of a pupil's desk. "This belonged to Miss Charlotte. I used to leave books and pamphlets for her." He actually *sat down* in the small seat.

"And all that lingered—" said Branwell.

"—was the unmistakable scent—" I added.

"—of the 'cigar-loving phantom!'" we both finished.

Monsieur then did something *never* described in *Villette*: he bent his massive head, covered his face with his hands, and actually started to sob! Branwell and I did not move. It was as if the Belgian Atlas had decided to shrug off the world.

I felt that I must act *now*, for a spare second could alter all.

"M. Heger," I asked, "why did you not answer Charlotte's letters? To her, this meant more than life itself."

"I know," he replied, his bearded face still masked. "I wished to—I knew her capacity for suffering. But it was . . ."

"Madame?"

He nodded, looking up. "She would read the letters in secret—even those addressed to me at the Athénée Royal. She did not wish me to provide . . . encouragement. I tried to protect Charlotte, and so tore up her letters. But my wife stitched them back together."

"That is madness!" Branwell cried.

"I suppose; I suppose that she wished to have 'proof' that the fault all lay on Charlotte's side—never mine." He removed a cloth handkerchief and wiped away his tears, some of which had fallen on his long dark *paletôt*.

"Why did you not write to Charlotte after Madame's passing?"

"I thought that . . . she must hate me for abandoning her to despair. We knew each other so long ago, and I thought—surely she would be wed—"

"*No.*" The wheels of my brain turned like those contraptions loved by Sir David. "Monsieur, if you do not act *now*, immediately and decisively, she is sure to marry another—"

"—whom she does not love—"

"—and who is wrong—unutterably wrong—for a being of her temperament!"

Monsieur seemed frozen in place.

"I tell you—there is not a moment to be lost. Already, we may be too late!"

M. Heger nodded. "I understand you. Still, all of this is overwhelming. I require some time—to think. There are six children to consider."

"Mon Dieu, Monsieur!" Not even Charlotte could evince my passion. "I thought *the French* were excitable and hasty, while the English plod on like a draught horse!"

His harsh features composed themselves into a sort of smile. "Please, do not allow me to detain you further. Journey back to *Angleterre* with the sure knowledge that you have performed your mission like two mighty *Napoléons!*"

He remained there, in that too-small chair, so consumed by memories that he did not rise to shake hands. Branwell and I let ourselves out and paused before the school.

"What in your opinion are the odds of his acting?" I asked.

"I am no great gambler—certainly not while sober— but I should say fifty percent. Or perhaps just the opposite!"

LIVING ONE'S OWN FICTION

Branwell and I began our return journey from Brussels. On the train, we attempted to determine possible outcomes.

"Will he come?" I asked impatiently.

"*You* were certainly correct as to the truth of his feelings. Henceforth I shall deem you 'Maria, Oracle at Delphi!'"

"Why does he not *act*?" I cried.

"He very well may. But as he says, he is hampered by a hundred children."

"Does he even know where Charlotte *lives*?"

"Of course. He wrote to Father, *begging* Charlotte to return as a teacher. A teacher of *what*, I ask you?" His eye bore a mischievous glint.

"I am beside myself!" I exclaimed. In truth, I was—I so wanted Charlotte to achieve her happiness that I *stood* all the way to Ostend.

We took the selfsame packet back to London, then two more trains to Keighley. Of course, snow was falling as if we were in the Urals. We walked in silence the four miles to Haworth, picking our way deliberately.

At last, for the first time in two years, I stood before the Parsonage door. The two of us clambered in, giving Tabby a genuine fright.

"Mista Branwell—for shi ah thowt theur wor dead!"

"Sorry to disappoint," he said merrily, dispensing a kiss atop her grey head.

"'N miss Marieur!"

I too gave her a kiss. "Where is Miss Charlotte?" I asked.

"Oh—shi is ' Bradf'd, squirin um gran' folks aroun'."

I looked to Branwell for a translation.

"And who are these grand folks, Tabby? That annoying Lord Shuttleworth who will not leave her alone?"

"Neya sir. These are 'em Smiths fra London village."

"Smith! What the devil is *he* doing here?" I cried, utterly shocking Tabby. She went off grumbling to the kitchen to fetch us a pot of tea.

Branwell shook his head. At that moment, someone knocked on the front door. In the absence of Tabby and Martha, I opened it.

"How do you do?" cried an exuberant, well-dressed woman. She nearly stepped through me on her way inside.

"Thankfully I am used to such storms from Manchester!" she proclaimed, removing her hat and coat and bending over the dining room fire. She looked at us. "I see that that gentleman is Branwell—oh yes, I have heard of his Irish hair! And you are . . . ?"

"Maria Shelby." I knew that I should have curtsied, or indulged in more formality, but there was something about this visitor that did *not* encourage politeness.

"Well! I am Mrs. Gaskell—you have most likely heard of me—"

I attempted to answer, but could not get out a word.

"—author of *Mary Barton*—"

I thought: *what a dreadful book—so didactic, and the heroine such a simpering, helpless doll . . .*

I nodded. Branwell had clearly not read it, for he looked at her with mystification.

"Currently, I have embarked on what is to be my *greatest* triumph: *The Life of Charlotte Brontë.*"

"But she is not dead!" I blurted.

Branwell laughed.

"No, of course not—but it *is* very probable she will soon go the way of her sisters—"

This was going too far! I wanted to order this officious woman back out on the snow.

"No doubt you are just *dying* to read a snippet—here!" She shoved some neatly written leaves directly into my hands. I read:

> Her honest plan for earning her own livelihood had fallen away, crumbled to ashes; after all her preparations, not a pupil had offered herself; and, instead of being sorry that this wish of many years could not be realised, she had reason to be glad. Her poor father, nearly sightless, depended upon her cares in his blind helplessness; but this was a sacred pious charge, the duties of which she was blessed in fulfilling.

And, about Brussels:

> . . . she resolved to compel herself to remain in Brussels till that [a knowledge of German] was gained. The strong yearning to go home came upon her; the stronger self-denying will forbade. There was a great internal struggle; every fibre of her heart quivered in the strain to master her will; and, when she conquered herself, she remained, not like a victor calm and supreme on the throne,

but like a panting, torn, and suffering victim. Her nerves and her spirits gave way.

"But none of this is true!" I cried. "Charlotte was *not* glad that her school 'failed' so she could take care of her father—and she was *not* happy to be home. By the bye, she *did* have a pupil: myself! And the reason she remained abroad is not at all what is limned here."

I handed the leaves back, but Mrs. Gaskell seemed unperturbed.

"I am not aiming at 'Truth,'" she said, "rather, at the rehabilitation of Currer Bell: instead of being coarse and contrary, we find the author pious, decorous, and a thoroughgoing lady. A lone figure wandering amidst the graveyard, I should say."

"Bollocks!" cried Branwell. "You may have described a fictional character, but you have *not* captured my sister."

Mrs. Gaskell smiled, availing herself of some cakes. "I know the *real* Charlotte Brontë, and it is of this woman that I write."

"You have turned her into Little Nell!" I exclaimed.

"So much the better to augment her reputation."

"Who *cares* what people think? 'When a true genius appears in the world, you may know him by this sign, that the dunces are all in confederacy against him.' Swift."

Mrs. Gaskell smiled and nodded—I do not believe she absorbed a single word. Branwell put a hand on my shoulder, for he knew that without constraint I might actually set upon her.

Our party increased twofold as the door opened *again*. Before us stood—wrapped against the weather—Charlotte, Smith, and his mother.

All concerned seemed astonished to witness the other.

"Elizabeth!" Smith cried to Mrs. Gaskell.

"Branwell!" Charlotte sobbed, throwing herself into his arms.

"Miss Shelby," Mrs. Smith said, nodding.

Once Charlotte had recovered from the sight of her brother, she ran over to embrace me. "Maria! How I have missed you. Would that you had been with me during my darkest hours."

"Be assured that the Light will always follow. I apologize for disobeying you and entering these doors. However, Mr. Branwell gave his permission."

"Do not think on it," she cried, "the Lord willing, the pestilence on this house has lifted."

I thought Mrs. Gaskell looked disappointed.

"How do you do, Miss Shelby?" Smith extended his hand.

"Very well, I thank you. What impelled you and Mrs. Smith to leave the comfort of London in the very dead of winter?"

"I desired to ascertain how my *favorite author* is faring."

"George!" Mrs. Gaskell reprimanded. I took it he was also her publisher.

I began to discern the motives for Smith's impromptu visit. He must have sensed that his personal connection to Charlotte had kept her on the writing path. Now that she had realized he had no romantic interest, his concern was for her output.

"Wherever is Mr. Brontë?" Mrs. Gaskell inquired. "After all of Charlotte's tales, I *do so* want to meet him."

To make him look ridiculous in your book, I reasoned.

"I shall fetch him." Branwell vaulted up the familiar staircase. "Papa!"

There followed loud decibels of relief as Branwell met Mr. Brontë. They both emerged minutes later accompanied by a solemn third figure: Mr. Arthur Bell Nicholls.

Introductions were made all around as Mrs. Gaskell did her best to charm the men.

"Mr. Nicholls!" she effused, sidling up to him and pumping his hand. "I hope, sir, that some welcome news follows this visit—*very* welcome, indeed!" She winked like an overly broad comic. So, Charlotte must have confided in her regarding Nicholls's proposal.

I held onto Branwell's arm as I looked at each person in turn: we were actually standing in the same room as Dr. John, Mrs. Bretton, one of the curates from *Shirley*, and—

M. Paul Emanuel!

Monsieur burst through the door, his *paletôt* swinging behind him. His face reflected agitation and—once he had surveyed the entire company—scorn.

"M. Heger!" Charlotte breathed, actually falling back as she clutched the edge of the table.

"Who?" asked Mrs. Gaskell.

I was so moved at seeing the two lovers reunited—after eight years! —knowing that it was *I*, Maria Shelby, who was the responsible party—well, I too had to clutch the dining room table.

I expected Monsieur to drop to a knee and propose to Charlotte on the spot. But he frustrated my ambition by giving Smith a dark scowl and an excited lecture in French.

"So, *this* is the intended. I should think you could find one more worthy, Miss Charlotte! This man is too young, while the phrenology of his forehead indicates that he is frivolous!"

"No, no, Monsieur—" Charlotte cried. She half turned toward Nicholls. "This is—"

"*Bébé doux Jésus, nous préserver!* What is this one—an undertaker? Explain to me, Miss Brontë, why I have journeyed across the sea merely to witness you playing coquette—to a *male harem*?"

He slammed back out the door into the frozen North. I idly wondered if Smith comprehended French.

"Who *was* that?" asked Mrs. Gaskell again. She looked disapproving, for this was *not* in keeping with her narrative.

The next one out the door was Charlotte. *Followed closely by me.* I had *not* come this far—spying on private correspondence, swooning over *Jane Eyre* and *Villette*, sailing to the Continent—to witness the utter collapse of *my* d_____d happy ending!

Branwell materialized at my side, but I ushered him away: this was a task for *a woman*! Though I was young and quick, and Charlotte small and frail, she knew her way through the moors almost as well as Emily, and I found I could not catch her. She vanished around a bend as I clumsily sped over snowdrifts. Once or twice, I nearly greeted them with my face, but at this crucial impasse, not even Winter could halt me!

I ran on over an endless, icy landscape, my breath laden with coughs, the cold assaulting my coatless form—still, no sight of Charlotte, and certainly not of Monsieur.

After a quarter of an hour, I simply had to rest, and doubled over to clutch my skirt. To *where* had they fled? Had she managed to secure him? Or was he at this moment fresh on his way back to Belgium?

I do not know what made me look up. Perhaps the advent of the winter sun from behind a cloud. Or the fresh fall of snowflakes: each individual, bearing a distinctive stamp, but melded together, indistinguishably joined.

That is when I saw them, atop a gentle hill. And thank G_d they *were* together, she almost invisible, wrapped in the folds of his long windswept coat.

I was too enervated to meet them and sat wearily down in the snow. No matter: they came to me.

"Tout va bien?" I asked, though I did not need a verbal assent. The look on Charlotte's face, though reddened from the cold—and even the one on Monsieur's— radiated pure joy.

Monsieur offered me his hand and carefully wrapped me in his long scarf. "To you I owe everything," he said in French. "My life, my happiness, my love! In what manner may I reciprocate this *unpayable* debt?"

"And I?" Charlotte asked shyly, snuggling inside his coat.

"Hmmm." I pretended to contemplate. "I believe I have conceived of a proper remuneration."

WEDDING THE SECOND

For once, there was a gathering at Saint Michael that did *not* involve an internment. This time, the black oak pews were filled, many with London notables: Thackeray, Gaskell, Smith, Lewes, and a certain Mary Ann Evans, seated by myself in a place of honor.

For the second time in as many years, I complemented a wedding party: this time as maid of honor. My fellow bridesmaids were Ellen, Charlotte's teacher old Miss Wooler, and one Marie Heger, aged all of sixteen. The best man was of course my accomplice both in love and crime: Mr. Branwell Brontë.

As I stood beside the altar, watching Charlotte progress down the aisle in her white embroidered dress ("She looks like a snowdrop!" Ellen exclaimed), I thought she had never been bolder than when all eyes were upon her. She seemed to glow beneath her veil as she approached her Edward Rochester—her M. Paul Emanuel.

The groom burst into unabashed sobs as he watched his intended approach. This time, there would be no Mason rushing in with news of a second living wife; no scheming Madame or shipwrecks to keep the two lovers apart. There were only great bouquets of flowers, imported from abroad; the tiny snowdrop bride; her trembling, black-suited groom; and tears from every guest, shed at last for joy and not from sorrow.

I could not conjecture the feelings of the curate, Mr. Arthur Bell Nicholls. After Charlotte had explained, gently, that the great love of her life had returned, he reacted at first with sulkiness, which evolved into quiet resignation. He even agreed to stay with Mr. Brontë as long as that gentleman should live. He was in the end a good man: merely not the *right* one, for which he is utterly blameless.

It was a true fairytale wedding. There were no awkward pauses or fumbled vows. I inclined my head to the left and perceived the family vault where Emily now lay silent; where Anne's name was inscribed though her bones lay far away.

I earnestly prayed that Anne in Heaven and Emily in Wherever She Was could bear witness to their sister's happiness. I knew that they would have approved, for Charlotte was not forced to "settle": instead, she attained her wildest Hopes and more.

It was somehow fitting that the true beginning and the end of a life occurred in the same sacred house. Anne would have praised God and Emily would have laughed. On this day, their presence was fully with me, and I am sure that Charlotte—now kissing the man she loved despite everything the world had thrown at her—felt the same twined souls invisibly at her side.

CODA

Reader, I am nearing the end of my tale.

It transpired that Charlotte and her Monsieur returned to Brussels to live. Charlotte had her hands full: managing her brood of step-children, the youngest being but six. I visited as often as I could, and what I saw was a changed woman: all the sorrows were submerged, and she bore a near perpetual smile.

She and M. Heger would walk the *allée défendue* behind the Pensionnat, delighting in past memories while forging a present and future together.

Mrs. Gaskell's *Life* never saw the light of day. At the wedding breakfast, I informed Smith bluntly that if such a pack of lies were published, it would not go unpunished: at least, not by me. Elizabeth Gaskell went on to become a successful novelist and could be heard all over London boasting of her "friendship" with Currer Bell.

Currer continued to thrive as Charlotte spent much of her time, when not devoted to family, writing: her next book being *Emma*. As literary muse, Monsieur stood in for Emily and Anne. Together, he, Charlotte, and young

Marie would pace around their dining room table, reading passages aloud—sometimes laughing with delight or groaning.

Since the newlywed couple had had their fill of teaching (especially Charlotte), *where* did they send their offspring to enjoy a sound education?

I believe it was to the B—— Establishment for Girls and Boys, situated in London in what had been a medieval monastery. Naturally, the interior was updated to make it cheerful for the pupils, and the range of subjects was wide—literature, geography, arithmetic, philosophy, and languages—offered to *all* regardless of sex.

This establishment has come to be known as that of a Thinking Person, and as I write in this year—1880—more families are sending their finest. The knowledge that the headmistress had been pupil to the three Brontës resonated with serious minds.

I am old now—in my fifty-fifth year—but my inner fire still burns. I no longer drop pails of water on the headmistress's head (considering that she is I), but I am not above dropping a book into some unsuspecting girl's desk.

I have taught so many now—including two who are nearest my heart. They were joined by Isabelle's three, placed by a recalcitrant Lord Nigel. When I am not about my duties, I sit down of an evening and write of my extraordinary life. This part you have already read, but there is so, so much more!

I have taken you now from my time as a spoiled young girl to my current standing as educator, writer—and woman of enterprise. Jane Eyre and Lucy Snow have reason to be proud.

But hold, you say . . . what of Branwell? Was his novel published, and did it gain fame for "Bertram Bell"? Indeed, Reader, it did. He became quite celebrated—the Bell triangle expanded to a square!—and spent the rest of his life writing, often with his first and best collaborator. Following his success, he never again relapsed, and has led an exemplary life as friend to Mr. Lewes and Miss Evans.

Am I forgetting some particular? Oh yes—what became of Branwell and me? Was the mad passion of our youth exchanged for a more mature, enduring love? Or, as with many first loves, did the force of feeling diminish, reduced to a blackened ember? I wish to keep certain matters private, but I *will* reveal that some months after Charlotte's bliss, an event transpired that permanently altered her brother.

Reader, I married him.